A EASTSIDE GANGSTA CHOSE ME

NIDDA

MZ. LADY P PRESENTS, LLC

❀ Created with Vellum

ACKNOWLEDGMENTS

First I would like to thank God for everything! Without him none of this would be possible. I would like to thank my parents for their love and support with everything. My aunt Lisa girl I owe you so much for never giving up on me and continuing to encourage me to keep going! & the rest of my family and friends that have been supportive I love y'all too! Mz Lady P for everything that you have done I will always be grateful! MLPP for being there to listen to my ideas and being supportive I appreciate y'all too!

To my readers I appreciate every one of you for giving me a chance! More is coming I don't plan on stopping anytime soon! S/O to Jay, Shay Shay, Janay, keyah, Mari, Tay and Rani! Y'all have all shown so much love!

KEEP UP WITH ME

FACEBOOK: NIDDA BIDDA

Facebook Reading Group: Nidda's Reading Spot
Instagram:_Nidda__
Twitter:_Nidda__
Thank you again! Don't forget to leave a Review.

COMING SOON:

MARRIED TO A BOSS SLEEPING WITH A
SAVAGE 2

Down To Ride For A Boss: Enforcer and Envii

KURUPT

"*P*lease stand and face the jury, Mr. Wright." Judge, Smith said. I got up and so did all three of my attorneys. I looked over at my baby Hope and sister Ahmina. They are all I have and I am all they have. I have to go home with them today and not to a ten by four cell. My baby was smiling and waving she is only three; she has no idea what is going on. Mina's eyes are full of tears I know she is scared that I'm gone and will not come with them today. I had to look away from them before I broke down and looked at the twelve people that had been judging me for the last six months. "Superior Court and the state of Colorado in the county of Denver; in the matter of State Colorado v. Kamal Dion Wright; case number CO916507211. We the jury in the above-entitled action found the defendant Kamal Dion Wright, not guilty of the crime of murder." The foremen read that was all the fuck I needed to hear all that other shit was a fucking formality.

I could hear my sister, with her loud ass. My palms are itching and I need to get out of here. I looked back at Mina and she wasn't crying anymore and my baby was clapping. The victim's family, on the other hand, was not as pleased. His bitch was screaming kicking and hollering being escorted out the courtroom. I listen to what the judge had to say and agreed to everything he wanted me to say okay to. He knows I murdered TP and it was due to the state and their bad choices and the police force and the way they mishandled the enormous amounts of evidence they had against me was the only reason I was walking out of here today. I do not give a fuck what the reason is as long as I am walking out. This will be my second case I have had to fight in the past three years, bitch I'm 2-0.

* * *

"Daddy!" Hope yelled as soon as she saw me and took off running towards me. Hope's mom left her with my sister when she was three months old and never came back. I tried looking for the bitch for a few days. Called all her people and nobody seem to know where she was at. To be honest I do not give a fuck whether the bitch dead or alive she doesn't give a fuck about my baby. Quita and I were never together. We were just fucking but when she got pregnant I did what I had to do to make sure she was good and did not want or need for shit. My money wasn't as long as it is now, but I always made sure that Quita was more than good. I do not understand what type of woman would just up and leave her child. I'm all my baby needs, I was there when she was born and I will be here as long as I live.

"I know you're happy to see Hope but can we go home now?" I heard Mina say, I was squeezing Hope so tight, shit I didn't realize for several minutes. "Shut up Mina, I missed yo big head ass too. Where the fuck is my car parked?" I said wrapping my free arm around Mina shoulder. We started walking towards my car. I was ready to get as far away from here as possible. Mina, hit the fob to unlock the car I looked in the direction of the beep. "Why the fuck are you driving this car, four other cars and this is what you been driving around town?" My damn brand new 2018, Black on black Porsche Panamera. I snatched my keys out of her hand and got Hope in her seat. When I opened the door, I was surprised it still looked and smelled brand new; I have only driven this car twice so she better had not been riding around in this car.

2

As I was getting in the car I noticed a thick bright yellow girl getting out of burgundy Caprice parked next to us. Baby, was thick as fuck wide hips and big ass thighs. She has brown shoulder-length hair. "Hi, how are you doing?" I said, at first I thought she was going to just ignore me. She must have found what she was looking for as she was rumbling through her purse. "Good." The woman said, dry as hell didn't even look at a nigga and walked away fast as hell. "Umm we ready to go home we been here all morning, we don't have time for you to be talking to random bitches in parking lots." Mina, said while honking the horn. I was watching baby walk away what a mutha-fucking sight to see. I pushed Mina's hands off the steering wheel "We are going home yall."

KAI MORAE

THAT NIGGA WAS BEING a little too damn friendly for me. I had to call into work to come get bail Deontae out of jail. This is the second time I have has to meet Tasha the bail bonds in the past twenty-four hours. Me doing this going to prove to him that I am down for him and soon everything will be good for us and all this bullshit will be in our past. My friend Katrina was calling but what I did not need to hear her fucking opinion today, or at least not right now because if I don't call her back the bitch will just keep on calling back to back.

"Sign right here," Tasha said, while looking at me like I had to be the dumbest bitch walking the planet. Lately, I have been feeling like everybody was looking at me like that because of all the shit that was going on with me and Deontae. It was always something every day it seems like it's a new fucking issue. When I met Deontae through my best friend Cariya, that nigga sold me a good dream. Everything that he told me was a damn lie. I got caught up and I just feel like I am in a dead end situation that I just can't get out of. The nigga made it seem like to me that he was getting big money and moving this and that. Come to find out after some time after we had started kicking it this nigga was moving another niggas bag and that was about a year ago and since then not much has changed.

More than anything I know that I stay around because I do not want the people that told me that he was not right for me and it was not going to work to win. I do have love for Deontae but I am not in love with him. He is just who is here. Deontae wants me and he says he loves me and I say it back not because I do but because it sounds good.

"Did you read through this?" Tasha asked, shit unless it has changed from yesterday bitch why would I need to read it again. Before, I could respond, she was off the bench where we were sitting and on her way to the back to get Deontae. So if I read it or not what's done is done. Cariya started texting me, so I texted her back and told her I would call her when I got home because I was driving. Cariya started calling I am sure just to see if I was going to answer for her because I didn't for Katrina.

After about ten minutes and three videos on Instagram, Deontae and Tasha made their way out. I was glad because I was ready to fucking go home already. "Wassup?" Deontae said, in between listening to Tasha read off all of the rules and regulations of the bond. I just wish they would not have given him a bond and he could have just had to sit for a few days. "Hey," I said, trying to sound like I was happy to see him and not irritated like I am. I had learned how to fake it really well since I have been dealing with Deontae. Deontae is about 5'7, light skin that is covered in tattoos, skinny, pretty white teeth and big brown eyes.

We made our way outside and to my car. I was so ready to just go home and relax these past two days have been stressful from dealing with Deontae and his shit, to my job and bullshit with school. I was stressed the fuck out and just wanted to go home. I was headed to my house and Deontae seemed to be so into whatever was going on his phone. "Aye take me by sisters. So I headed to Jalisa's house. Jalisa is cool, I guess. I only fucked with her because of D otherwise we would not talk. We don't have anything in common. She cool when she wants to be;

done fucked half the community but always trying to give me advice on what I need to do with my relationship. I didn't want to go to Jalisa's but I was not in the mood to argue either so I just made my way over there.

"What's yo problem?"

"Nothing, I'm good."

That was a lie; I'm tired of being in this situation. I don't want to be with him anymore. Having to deal with his mom, sisters and then him and his bullshit is just too much. I just want him to leave me alone because I can't just walk away, but if he does shit it can just be over. I don't think it's going to happen because a nigga will never leave his dummy.

* * *

"YOU NEED to settle down and get serious with Kai, look how she's been there for you. She is always is there for you." Jalisa said, while they mom Gina cosigned with her. I tolerated them because I had to because I was with D but they both are fake as fuck and I know just as fast as they tell him this about me, it wouldn't take much for them to say the same shit about another bitch. It doesn't surprise me I knew Gina wasn't shit the first time I met her she took a handful of Percocet's and that should have told my ass the whole family wasn't right. I just walked out the kitchen because I wasn't in the mood to pretend and went into the living room and played with Amir, Jalisa's son who was lying on cover in the middle of the floor.

"Deontae really does love you, Kai," Jalisa said, as she walked in the room. This bitch must want a ride somewhere or want something because why she insists on talking about this shit today. This is the same bitch that less than twenty-four hours ago told me to get some-body on the side until Deontae got his shit together. "I love him too, I forced myself to say. My friends were blowing up my phone so I just powered it off. "Hey, are you going stay over here I need to use the car right quick and shoot this move with Memphis." Deontae said I rolled my eyes so hard I felt like they were going to pop out my fucking head. I should have ignored his momma and sister calls when he was in jail.

"I'm going home," I said as I handed Jalisa Amir and walked out the house. I did not bother saying bye to anybody. Gina raised this grown ass boy and Jalisa is all for him and all of his bullshit. I was a fucking ATM and car to this nigga nothing more and nothing less. I knew it wouldn't take long before we got to this shit. So he'll be out with Memphis all night and I am supposed to sit at home by myself until whenever he decides to come back. If I see the muthafucka before the sun comes up it would be miracle.

"I'm not going to be gone long, I'll be out for a few hours and I'll be home," Deontae said that was just for me to not say anything. We had made it to the car, I was in the driver seat and D was in the passenger seat. "I'm over this shit; it is always the same shit. Damn not one whole day without this shit!" I screamed, I hardly ever said anything I just let Deontae do as he pleases just in an attempt to keep him around. Doesn't anybody else want me and a piece of man is better than no man at all? I keep telling myself but this shit ain't working for me no more. The confidence I once had, ambitions, dreams, and goals seemed to have all went the fuck away since I have been fucking with this nigga. "Fuck it I'll get me another bitch!" Deontae said, as he got out and slammed my car door. I burned rubber to get the fuck away that muthafucka. He thought I was going to chase him; it was not going to happen not today. That is the fucking problem all I have done is chase in behind this nothin ass nigga since I met him.

KURUPT

I WAS TRYING to enjoy being home and spending time with Mina and Hope because tomorrow before the sun come up its back to business and I gotta hit the ground hard as hell for all the time I missed. Standing on the balcony attached to my room looking over my estate. A few niggas thought that I was gone and was not coming home. So they did as they pleased and had no intentions to give me what was mine.

I heard a loud ass muthafucka downstairs; I knew it was Enforcer loud ass. E and I have been friends all of our lives are moms were best friends. We were born three days apart. Gotti and Enforcer are the only two people outside my family that I trust with my life. These niggas never switched up and their names can't be found on any nigga paperwork. They know shit that I wouldn't tell anybody but God. They made sure Hope and Ahmina were good while I was gone and if it ever happens again, I know they will be right there again. I worked my ass off to get off the block and I'm not going back. I made my way downstairs to holla at E.

"Welcome home my nigga!" E said as he walked towards me. We dapped up and walked into one of the living rooms. Hope and Ahmina were watching TV in the living room right outside the kitchen. I gotta do something for her because I know she been putting her own life on hold to be there for Hope and I want her to know that I appreciate it. Since I'm home after I handle a few things. She and Hope will be my only priorities. E and I made our way down the hall. E, sat on a bar stool that wrapped around the bar that took up a whole wall in my game room. I turned on all the TV's. E is a smooth ass nigga, but deadly. He is loud as hell all the fucking time and his wife Envii is definitely for him. She the only person I know that can get him to shut up and follow instructions. E is always brushing his fucking hair, even right fucking now like he got somewhere to be.

E is loyal as fuck and when I was a broke ass nigga he was right there. So it's only right that sense, we've come up and are a long way from them corner days that he is here still. "Hey now that your home what's up first?" E said, while pouring a shot of Cîroc. I know he just wanted the word to tear some shit up, but we have to take shit slow I just got out. "Nigga, slow down them niggas ain't going anywhere. Will handle business in the morning, nigga yo gun will still shoot in the morning." I said, while hitting his shoulder and making my way to my chair. "Alright K, that nigga got one more night to live." E said, before taking his shot to the head. Hope came running in the game

7

room. Looking at her made me think about I couldn't do this shit forever and I was going to eventually have to get out the game and settle down.

Quaneisha had been calling me since I powered on my phone. We met a few years ago one night when I was out with E and Gotti at the club. Quaneisha is bad bitch Carmel complexion, long legs, long jet black hair that's all hers. Big brown eyes and baby face. Quaneisha talks too damn much but I tolerated it though because she was cool. I brought her around Hope and my baby hated her. I didn't like the fact that she kept trying to tell her no, stop and don't do that. After about a half an hour of that Hope just started screaming. She screamed at the top her lungs until the bitch left an hour later. Quaneisha looked out while I was locked up; she answered every time I called, wrote me letters and came to visit me. With Hope not fucking with her I don't think it could ever work. Even with that, I had every intention of fucking her tonight.

The only people that know where I live are Gotti, E, and Quaneisha. I got a notification that somebody was coming in the main door on the TV. I knew it was Gotti him and E had keys. Gotti walked into the room "Uncle Gotti!" Hope screamed as she ran up to Gotti to hug him. Most kids would be scared as hell of this nigga Gotti but not Hope. This nigga is about 6'8 black as the night, as wide as the doorway he just came through and I've seen his appearance intimidate some of the biggest gangsters I know. Let alone what his trigger finger does. "Welcome home!" Gotti said as he walked up to me I got up to dap him up. As I did that Quan name ran across the TV, now she was calling the house.

Instantly, Hope started crying. She isn't a crybaby but she is spoiled as hell and I haven't ever told her no. She just does not fuck with Quaneisha. E and Gotti started killing their self-laughing. "I think old girl the devil K, kids like everybody and Hope is a friendly baby but she doesn't even want to see Quaneisha name on the caller id cuz." E said, while pouring a shot. I laughed as I picked up Hope. It was time for her to go to bed; she laid her head on my shoulder and held on tight to my arm but did not stop crying until Quaneisha went to the answering machine.

"Look at that shit Kurupt; it's time to find somebody new the family has spoken." Gotti, said, talking like he was one of them niggas in the mob even attempted their accent. "Fuck y'all niggas!" I said, as I went and put Hope to bed. "Look what Quan put on Facebook?" Ahmina said, as I came down from putting Hope down while putting her phone up to my face. It read daddy's home. "That bitch is dumb you haven't even answered any of her phone calls. The bitch is delusional." I mushed Mina's face and gave her phone back.

* * *

"GOOD MORNING! OPEN THE DOOR." I said and then hung up. It was a little after two in the morning. E and Gotti had just left and we discussed the plans for today but I need to see Quan before I got business. I had two dozen of red roses in my hand and a box from my jeweler in my other hand. Mina didn't like the bracelet, so I was going to have to give it somebody. Quan wasn't my bitch and more than likely never will be but if I fuck with you I fuck with you. When she opened the door the smile that spread across her face was what I was hoping for instead of a discussion about why I didn't answer her calls. She hugged me so tight and started kissing all over my face. She moved from in front of the door so I could come in.

Quaneisha had on a dark light blue lace bra and thong panty set and I couldn't help but watch the way her ass shook and she took the roses in the kitchen to put them in water. I sat down on her thot furniture. You know the brown sectional with the chase that most thots own that's the furniture she has in her one bedroom condo downtown. Quan came back into the living room and stood in front of me. It was still pitch black outside but the street light was shining in from her balcony and hitting her body just right so that I could see everything that I want to see. "Come here." I said as I grabbed Quan by her hands and pulled her onto my lap. Quan's pussy was okay, it wasn't the wettest, I've had wetter and it wasn't the tightest I've had tighter but her head was the best I've ever had.

Quaneisha was on my lap I was running my finger through her hair. "How has everything been? How was work? How is your mom doing?" Even though Quaneisha and I did not have a future together I still considered us to be friends and I truly do care about her and how's she doing. We talked for a few minutes about how everything was going. How much she hated her job and wanted to go back to school.

Quan hopped off my lap and sat right in between my legs. Unzipping my pants and pulling them down in one swift motion. Grabbed my shit with both hands and went to work. All you could hear was Quaneisha slurping on my shit. I looked down at Quan in amazement; this bitch had perfected this shit so well. After licking up my shit and running her tongue around the tip a few times she swallowed my shit hole. She took the whole 10 without a muthafucking problem. I felt like I was about to come and I'm sure Quan did too the way I pumping in her mouth as hard as I could and gripping the shit out her hair. She could go the shop tomorrow all on me. She popped my dick out and went to sucking on my balls. I laid my head back and close my eyes and bit my bottom lip "Damn Quan. Fuck!" I managed to get out in between moaning and groaning and that shit made Quan go even harder on my shit. After about fifteen minutes I came long and hard and Quan caught all that shit and didn't waste none of all of it went down her throat.

Quan got up off her knees licking her lips and grabbed me by my hands, as I stepped out Gucci shoes and Givenchy jeans and lead the way to her room. "Welcome home baby," Quan said, as I grabbed her by her waist as made our way down the hall.

KAI MORAE

I can't get in touch with Deontae a few hours my ass, he came to my house last night and he knows today I have to go to Rissa's funeral. Rissa was my childhood best friend. She overdosed about a week ago and this nigga just does not care. I tried to call Deontae again for the hundredth time and his phone was still going to the answering machine. I tried to call Caryia because I would just rather not hear Katrina's mouth but she did not answer. I sat back down on the couch because it was clear that I was not going anywhere anytime soon unless this nigga showed up. How the fuck did I end up here, I thought to myself.

No dick is that good to be willing to let somebody disrespect and use you. No, Deontae isn't beating my ass but the way that I feel about myself has a lot to do with him and the way he treats me and the way he talks me. I try not to even look at myself in the mirror because I just do not like what I see anymore. I'm so disgusted with myself and this horrible relationship I'm in is not making it any better. When did I become so damn dumb? I graduated high school the top of my class just two years ago. I started out on the right track decided to go to community college. Since I have been fucking with D in a matter of

11

months I am damn near failing all of my classes and if I have a job on Monday I'll be surprised. I need to be with somebody that loves and motivates me to do better and it seems that all Deontae does is just drag me down.

* * *

I ENDED up crying myself to sleep and woke up; to my phone ringing it was now nine at night. Rissa's funeral was long over and D was calling. "I'm out fucking side man hurry the fuck up!" D yelled into the phone and hung up. Like, I wasn't the one that should have been mad. Rissa's funeral is something that I can't go to tomorrow or reschedule like I have had to do with everything else in my damn life since I met this nigga. I made my way outside to my car. Soon as the car door shut Deontae, started you been blowing me up all morning and then it takes you forever to come outside. "You the reason I lost all my fucking money!" Deontae screamed while hitting the dashboard and started driving like a maniac in my damn car. When he hit the dashboard, it made me jump.

I didn't even waste my time responding to his last comment that just made him even madder. I can't do this shit anymore, this is it. "You never loved me anyway; I'm going to get me another bitch that does more than what you do for me. You are not here for me and you don't do all that you can. A real woman would be all the way there for me. What type of woman are you?!" Deontae screamed as he slammed the car into park he had made it to his drop off destination. It's only so much that I can take and today out of all days I can't take this shit.

I do not know what I had been thinking missing Rissa's funeral was the final straw and this muthafucka hasn't said anything about that. He wants to talk about some money that his bad luck ass lost gambling and where the fuck did come right back to. To gamble some more, I guess I'm supposed to go into my purse and give him more money to lose. Fuck the two bonds that I have paid for the last day, none of that shit matter.

"Fuck you! I'm done another bitch can have you and yo fake

through so much bullshit before Deontae ever came in the picture. Getting kicked out of school, fighting, running away and all types of other bullshit was a regular for me. During my teenage years, I caused her hell and all of my other family was telling her to let me go to the state, but she wouldn't give up on me.

The door is always unlocked, so I let myself in. "That's going to be you right there," my aunt said. I turned to look at the TV and it was a woman sitting on the curb in handcuffs. My aunt doesn't know about any of the stuff that I do on the side, but she has heard about the stuff that Deontae has done. I didn't want to argue with her today, so I just didn't say anything. I went to the table, where a stack of mail was sitting. I was waiting for the decision if I could get back into CCD. I found the envelope; I was looking for and opened it. I had fucked up bad and failed so many classes, I lost my financial aid and shit just been all bad ever since. Luckily the letter said I could enroll again on a probationary period. I had to have a meeting and sign an agreement before I can actually enroll in school.

"Is that what you were looking for?" My aunt asked.

"Yea, they are giving me a second chance."

Even though I don't live with my aunt anymore, I never changed my address. My aunt just wants what is best for me and I have apologized for so many times for all my bullshit, she sacrificed so much for me. She has a son, B and he is fifteen. He is the exact opposite of me he is a good kid and does everything the right way.

"Kai, I just want what's best for you. You can do all the things that you want to do, but you have to leave that boy alone."

"I know Aunt Lisa and I am. I'm going back to school and I'm getting everything back on track."

"Rodney called me earlier, looking for you."

I know Rodney didn't tell her too much, but she is very dramatic so whatever he did tell her is too damn much. Between Rodney and Deontae's other family telling her shit, no matter what I say she's going to try to hear me out. She was still talking about how bad of a person Deontae is. Everything she is saying is true, but this is exactly why I do not come around. I understand that she doesn't agree with my decisions, shit I can admit I've made a lot of mistakes. I don't want to talk about all the negative and wrong things that I have done.

"Alright, auntie I'll see you later."

I didn't waste my time responding to none of the shit she was saying. I was going to have to show her the change in order for her to believe me. I have every intention to show her and prove to myself that I can get my life back on track.

* * *

KATRINA and I are getting pedicures and I was looking at my choices for classes, for next semester. Katrina was complaining about her nigga, well he is not her man but that's none of my business. I would agree or say something every few minutes but I wasn't really listening. She always got a damn problem, ask your opinion on what she should do and turn around and do what she wants to do. Katrina is short, thick, chocolate and has hair that touches the middle of her back. She has hazel eyes and is really pretty, but she is so damn scandalous.

"How are you doing?" I heard someone say and I looked up.

It was the nigga from the mall that was all in my damn business. What the fuck is he doing in the nail shop? I waved and put my attention back on my phone. He is fine though, I didn't really pay him any attention the other times I saw him. He is Chocolate, tall and a nice ass body. He has big brown eyes and a low haircut, neatly trimmed goatee. I had to clench my thighs together, to slow down the throbbing that was happening between my legs.

"You too pretty to be so damn mad," the man said.

"What's yo name?" I asked, while looking up at him.

"Kamal, but everybody calls me Kurupt," Kamal said, extending his hand.

I shook, his hand, hoping he would just leave me the fuck alone. I don't have time or the energy for no ain't shit nigga. Unless he is here getting his nails done, I'm sure he is here with a bitch. I was just waiting for a mad bitch to come storming over here. He just stood in front of me staring.

"I'm ready, come on. She doesn't want you." A girl said, smiling at me hitting Kamal on the arm.

"You should call me sometime?" Kamal said.

"I'm sorry, I can't do that," I said, with Katrina hitting my arm.

I needed to get my shit back together; no nigga was going to ever get me off my track again. I didn't have any more time to waste. I could have been done with undergrad by now, but naw I was chasing in behind Deontae I'm not looking for nigga right now. Kamal, just walked away. So whoever that girl was must not have been his bitch, or she was just cool with her nigga bopping around the town.

"You are dumb as fuck. Why wouldn't you take his number?" Katrina said.

I rolled my eyes; I don't need advice from somebody else about a nigga that doesn't have one. Listening to her I would have been fucking half the city. My phone started ringing, I looked down it was Deontae again. I sent him to voicemail and went back to listening to Katrina.

* * *

I KNOW it was late because I went to sleep after midnight. My phone was ringing and I was feeling in my bed trying to find it.

"Hello," I said

"Kai, you have to get up to the hospital, Deontae can't breathe," Gina Deontae's mom said.

I didn't say anything even though I need to be done with him. I don't want him to die. I sat up and leaned against the headboard.

"Kai!" Gina screamed.

"I'm on my way," I said and hung up.

I just needed to go make sure that he was okay. So I got up and threw on some clothes and made my way to the hospital. As I made my way to the hospital, I kept telling myself that I had to come up to the hospital because it was the right thing to do. I had to put my feelings aside for a minute until I knew that he was okay. As I pulled up to the hospital and I saw Kyra pulling up so I knew it was going to be a long night.

I got my ass out the car since I bought my ass all the way here. I wasn't looking forward to being in the same room with Kyra. She is Deontae's baby momma and the crazy thing is we've never had words with each other. We'll be in the same room and not say shit to each other but when I'm not around this bitch always has a lot to say. That's my problem with her rat ass. She is the most irritating bitch to ever walk earth. She'll call asking Deontae, to come and get water off the top shelf. Um bitch, how the fuck did it get up there? I don't blame her because Deontae bought this bitch into the picture.

As I walked into the emergency room I noticed Jalisa and Omari. I made my way over to where they were sitting. I sat down next to Omari, even though she is Deontae's sister I can honestly say she has always kept it real with me unlike the rest of their family. Kyra walked into the emergency room and sat across from us. She spoke to Jalisa and Omari but just looked at me. This is nothing new.

"Come back here," Gina said as she walked up on us.

Kyra jumped up, she just knew that Deontae wanted to see her. I knew that Gina, wasn't talking to her she was looking dead at me. I'm sure she didn't call Kyra up here. I'm sure this is all Jalisa messy asses doing. I was getting ready to take my ass home, he must be doing okay, and Gina's done crying and everybody else is cool and calm.

"Girl, you know Deontae does not want to see you. Come on Kai," Gina said.

I got up, but as I did I decided this will be my last time answering their phone calls I would have a new number in the morning. Kyra or whoever else could have this shit. Everything was turning around for me and getting caught up in Deontae's shit would only derail my plans. I rolled my eyes as I followed behind Gina, to Deontae's room. I just wanted to go home and get in my bed; this nigga is not dead or dying!

Deontae was lying across the room in a hospital bed; I sat in the chair across the room. Deontae was hooked up to a breathing machine. Gina got on the hospital phone calling somebody. All this bitch does is talk, who the fuck could she need to talk to and it's almost three in the morning. Deontae started motioning for me to come here. I hesitated, but I walked over to the bed.

"I'm surprised to see you here?" Deontae said, while moving the mask off his face.

"Yo baby momma out there you want me to go get her for you?"

"Hell naw! Fuck that bitch! Why is she even here?" Deontae said and started choking.

Kyra has been the biggest headache. Considering the fact that her daughter is not even here yet; I can only imagine what the bitch will be like when the baby gets here. This nigga fucked and sucked her since we've been together. I should have left his ass alone after Jalisa accidentally told me Kyra was pregnant.

"I'm sorry Kai, on me Kai. I am and I love you" Deontae said, while grabbing my hand.

As much as I hate to admit it; I miss D it's not all bad and we do have good days. The bullshit, we've been going through here lately I can't deal with. The peace of mind that I've had since I haven't been talking to him I can't let him take that away from me. The bad has been outweighing the good and I can't do this shit. Nobody else wants me though and Deontae always comes back. We might take a break here and there but he always comes back.

KURUPT

"Come on K! What are you doing?" Mina yelled.

I was looking at the college bitches. I should have gone to college. It's some bad bitches here. Mina already knew what this was going to be when she asked me to come up here with her. Mina has me up here at the Metropolitan University of Denver. She has to get her books; classes will be starting soon. While I was fighting my case she put it on hold to be there for Hope. That shit bothered me, but I know that Mina will do anything for Hope and me.

Before Hope was born it was just me and Ahmina. Alice kicked me out on the day I turned sixteen. Her boyfriend didn't want me there anymore. So in order to keep her man, I had to go. I vowed to go back and get Mina as soon as I got right to go back and get Mina and I did that. Alice would do anything to keep a man around, so I knew it wouldn't be too long before she was kicking Ahmina out. I gave myself ninety days to get right and I went from sneaking and selling weed when I was living with Alice to taking over fat Ricky's block. Alice damn near pushed Mina out the house; when I came back to get her. Mina was only twelve years old at the time.

I've come a long way since then. Everything that I do is for Hope and Mina. There is nothing that I wouldn't do for them. I'm going to make sure they have the best and have all the opportunities that I didn't have growing up. I am thankful that Ahmina has chosen a different lifestyle than the one I did. Even though she wants to be the damn police; I still support her.

"Mina, damn you really are trying to be the police," I said while looking through the books as she laid them on the counter.

"No, I'm not! Shut up! These classes are required."

Hope was waking up; she had been sleeping in the stroller since shortly after we got here. I paid the cashier for the books and got my baby out the stroller. Mina and this damn university are taking all my damn money today. Why are these fucking books so damn high? For Mina, anything but damn. Good thing its pay day! My phone was vibrating in my pocket, I looked and I had a message from Envii: I'm bout to make yo favorite dish! That's just what I had been waiting to hear.

"I'm hungry K," Mina said.

"Get something Ahmina and get Hope something too," I said as I sat down at a table in the Tivoli.

I was ready to get the fuck out of here. The work was in and I need to go as soon as we made it through this orientation. Mina has one friend Modesty, Gotti's little sister but she not friendly so nobody trying to be her mean ass friend.

"She is so, cute." A Woman said, I looked up and it was yellow.

"Thank you. What is your name?"

"Kai," Yellow said and walked away.

I can't lie yellow is fine but it's something else about her. I think it's the fact that she's not throwing it at me is what makes me want to know more about her. I have bitches throwing it at me at me all day long but yellow ain't thinking about me. I keep running into her and I never seen her before the day I got out. So I know that she ain't out here bad or ran through because I never heard anybody mention her. Kai must have a broke, lame ass nigga.

KAI MORAE

WHAT ARE the chances that I keep running into Kamal? I had come to pick up my books and just finished up with that long ass early session for orientation. Deontae was waiting for me outside and I was actually happy for the first time in a while. Everything has been going well. Before I started fucking with Deontae I was selling crack, but I hid it from Deontae because I didn't think no nigga would want to fuck with me if they knew I was doing that. With Deontae, I didn't tell him because he doesn't have a hustling bone in his body. Some shit you can't teach and he just doesn't get it. Even with working it's still not enough for me. So I haven't stopped yet, but once I finish school and get a good job I'm done for good.

"Where you get this from Kai?" Deontae asked as I got in the car.

He was holding the t-shirt I was supposed to be dropping off to fat Ricky before I came to the school, but I was already running late. I thought I had it in my fucking purse. I couldn't tell him it was mine.

"It's my cousin Shod's, I was supposed to be dropping it off for him before I picked you up, but I needed to get to Orientation on time."

"This all he gave you,"

I had been doing so good keeping this away from Deontae and now, he wants to know if I have more. Is this nigga smoking crack now? I wanted to keep my business and personal separate because combining the two could fuck me in the end, while he goes on his fuck merry way.

"Naw, I got a little more."

"Alright, we need to go the house and I can handle this for you."

* * *

"I'M with my nigga Memphis, I swear I'm on my way, Kai," Deontae said.

I'm sitting at home waiting for him to get back. He was taking too damn long for me. Something about Memphis I did not like him from the first time I met his ass. Memphis is caramel complexion, skinny and looks like a fucking bug. Something about him just screams police to me. I've spent a lot of time around niggas from the streets and this nigga ain't right. I always felt uncomfortable around him and he was always staring at me.

"Alright, hurry up."

"Alright, baby I'll be there in a minute. I love you."

Before I could lay my phone down, I got a text message. Stop by right quick, the pill lady said. I happened to be getting ready to pass her house, so I jumped off the exit. I have been fucking with her for a minute. Monica is my Aunt Lisa's friend, but she doesn't know about my business that I don't receive a W-2 from. Monica is cool when she wants to be. Monica runs a daycare out her house. I'm sure the state or her clients don't know what else she is doing in her house. When I got to the door, before I could knock it swung open. Monica is Carmel complexion, short, chunky with a big ass. She's pretty, but not as pretty as she thinks she is and because I know she's scandalous that makes me even more careful when dealing with her. She's desperate for some money because she's texting me.

"You're not working today?" I asked.

"Naw, not today I need a break."

Monica is deep in debt but works whenever she feels like it. That's why her clients always leave because she's not reliable. She can tell you what club is popping tonight, but I wouldn't let the bitch watch my dog let alone my child.

"How many you got?"

I don't have all damn day. Monica handed me a bottle. I looked at the label it was 120 Percocet's. I was looking at her crazy; she always sold me her sons Adderall. I could get rid of these and this bitch swears she so damn book smart, but she has no idea how much these go for.

"You don't have any more Adderall?"

"Yea, here they go. I need a hundred dollars for my lights."

I placed the hundred dollars on the table and made my way out the door. Nothing else mattered. The Percocet's alone we're going to give me money back and some and how I normally overcharge the dumb muthafuckas. Monica was saying something but didn't matter what I that was all she was getting. The sad thing is she didn't have a clue about this shit but wanted to be involved so bad. Bitches fuck one nigga that sell drugs and swear they a trap queen. All I could do is shake my head.

* * *

I woke up out of my sleep, my phone was ringing. It was a number I didn't know and it was almost midnight. I answered it and it was D. He was drunk as hell. I could tell by the way he was talking and I was not ready to deal with his drunk ass. I mean there is nothing wrong with having an occasional drink every now and then but if you have to drink every day just to get by you have a problem. Being around this nigga when he was drunk made me not want to drink at all.

"Aye, come outside for a minute," Deontae said.

"Here I come."

I threw on a shirt and some jogging pants and made my way outside. I didn't want Deontae drunk ass being too loud for my damn neighbors before somebody is complaining. Deontae was getting out of Memphis truck as I made my way out of my building. I live in Cherry Creek Greens. It's a bunch of fucking Mexicans and of course they all outside tonight. Memphis, headlights, was shining in my damn face, but I could see Memphis's knockoff glasses and his beady eyes. Fucking staring at me is making me uncomfortable and I guess Deontae too drunk to realize.

"Come on D, its cold out here."

"I love you, Kai."

"I love you too D, come on," I said, grabbing his arm.

I was trying to stop his drunk ass from smacking the concrete. His pale skin, skin is red. When we got into the apartment Deontae went to get in the shower and I went back to bed. I needed to try to get some sleep and go to Netflix in the morning and I can't be late. I told Deontae I would let him finish selling rest of what I had, but that was a lie.

* * *

I WOKE UP SHORTLY AFTER; I finally got back to sleep with Deontae's head in between my legs. Giving head is not his thing. I don't know it's like he doesn't know what he's doing. His kisses are trash too. His dick makes up, for the head. I pretended to be pleased for about two minutes and faked a nut. Then I sat up straight and started pulling down D's boxers. He was already hard and started to rub the tip against my other set of lips and eased his dick inside my warm and wet box.

Deontae pulled me damn near off the bed and was stroking too damn slow for me. As I began to roll my eyes, he started to pick up the pace, while taking his index finger and rubbing it on my clit. Deontae was hitting my spot and I was throwing it right back.

"Is this my pussy Kai?"

"Yes!" I screamed out as I came.

Deontae flipped me over on my stomach, while still inside of me. He was beating my box from the back and I was rubbing his balls. D was smacking my ass and pulling my hair. That caused me to cum again and D came shortly after.

* * *

I'M WAITING for Deontae to come and get me from work and of course, he's fucking late. I already had an attitude from this stupid ass job and now he just has to be late. He was on his way ten minutes ago; all I want to do is just go home. I checked my phone and I had a text message from my people asking for their favorite dish and that made me even madder; now I'm missing out on money.

I looked up and Deontae was pulling into the parking lot and somebody was in the passenger seat. Once he got closer I saw that it was Toni and that just made even more irritated. As they pulled up to where I was standing, I rolled my eyes. Toni jumped out and got in the back seat. I noticed that there were bags from the mall in the backseat. So all the money that this nigga has made he has spent at the mall; I assumed once I got in the car.

"So, you went shopping?" I asked.

"Yea, just something light nothing serious," Deontae said, rubbing his hand on my thigh.

I just wanted this nigga out of my car, so I could go make some money. I was trying not to have an attitude, but it wasn't working. I turned up Yo Gotti's "Juice" as loud as it could go. I wanted to get away from this nigga as far as I could. I have never met a nigga so damn dumb in all my life. Here I am, stuck fucking with his dumb ass.

"So you, got a fucking attitude?" Deontae asked as he put the car in park.

Toni hoped his broke ass out the car. He didn't have any bags in his hands. He just a real live bum and this nigga next to me is just as broke as him. The only reason he has a dime in his pocket or these fucking shoes in my back seat is from out of my bag. What the fuck have I done to deserve to be stuck with nigga?

"Come on, just get it out I gotta go."

My mind was on my money and nothing else since I now see that this time is no different. The only difference is this time it was my work that he sold and tricked off, for some clothes and a Jordan's. He could keep the little money that I know he had left and that's exactly why I didn't give him the whole thing. Every nigga is not meant to sell drugs and Deontae is one of those niggas. D got his shit out the back seat and slammed my door. Shit, I should be the one mad. Here this nigga go acting like a bitch! I didn't have time for this shit; I needed to make my way to Fat Ricky.

* * *

As I came out of Fat Ricky's; I noticed Memphis truck parked in the driveway two house's down. I just hoped that Deontae wasn't in the truck. Somebody was screaming "Ayye!" I kept on fucking walking, that ain't my damn name. I needed to shoot a few more moves and take my ass home. I made it to my car and replied to Cariya text message telling her I would be over in the morning. Since shit was going well with me and D, I haven't hung out for a while but that's out the window. As I drove by where Memphis was parked he was getting out his truck trying to flag me down. I kept the fuck going, he doesn't have shit that I want. He's Deontae's friend, not mine. I looked down at my phone and it was number I didn't know calling, but I answered it.

"Hello," I said.

"Damn baby you couldn't stop, you just going to keep on driving." Memphis said.

So, niggas save other niggas bitches numbers after they use their phone now? I was even more annoyed that this nigga is calling me baby. Bitch I'm not your baby! Niggas got whole families and don't mind cutting into the next bitch for some pussy.

"What do you want Memphis?"

"You need to fuck with a real nigga like me; I'm the type of nigga that you need in yo life."

"Yea Memphis I'm straight. As you already know I have a man."

I hung up on his ass and made my way to get the rest of my money from Alice.

* * *

"ARE YOU AND MEMPHIS STILL COOL?" I asked as I flipped over the chicken.

"Naw, that nigga been on some bullshit. Why?" D said he was sitting at the dining room table bagging up.

"He called me trying to get with me, earlier."

Deontae started going the fuck off. I've never seen him act like this before. Something was telling me that it was because of whatever was going on with him and Memphis more than him trying to fuck with me. "That nigga is a real, bitch! What the fuck did that nigga say?" Deontae screamed. Not really wanting an answer he just needed something else to say. He was dialing somebody's number must have been Memphis's.

"So, you were trying to get with my girl?" Deontae said.

I went back to the kitchen and checked on my food. Deontae was acting like a bitch and I didn't tell him about Memphis for him to call

29

him and argue with him on the phone. I had more important shit to worry about than Memphis and Deontae's issues with each other. I took my chicken out and went and grabbed my kindle and started back reading B Capri's *A Jackboy Stole My Heart*. Deontae was still screaming at the top of his lungs at Memphis.

KURUPT

"Quan, get the door!" I yelled down the stairs.

I don't know who that could be? Quan is cool, but I just need to let her go find the man that's right for her. I just came by to grab something and I should have left her in the car because Hope is screaming. She's not going to be trying to hear that but this is coming to an end. As I made my way downstairs, I heard somebody yelling and screaming. What the fuck is going on? I know this bitch Quan not arguing with Mina?

"Get the fuck off me!" Mina was screaming and somebody was standing over her hitting her all in her fucking face. She was kicking and attempting to hit them but they are getting her ass. I ran down the stairs and pushed the muthafucka out the house, they were standing in the doorway and the door is wide open. I helped Mina off the ground and Mina, was trying to get out of my grasp to get to this bitch, that had jumped on her.

"Mina, I got it, go in there for a minute!" I said, getting even madder than I already am.

"You are just going to throw yo momma out yo house like I'm some bitch on the streets?" Alice said.

I haven't seen her since the day I went to get Mina and if I did I wouldn't have noticed her. Her voice, I will never forget though. She used to be beautiful, with a caramel complexion, long think sandy brown hair. Now she just looks like every other crackhead I know. How the fuck does she know where I live? How the fuck did she get past the gate? Alice was standing in the doorway waiting for an answer. I walked outside, brushing past her and shut the door behind me.

"You need to go. You are not welcome here."

Alice lit up a Newport and leaned against my home. I always wondered how I would feel if I saw her again. She made her decision a long time ago as far as I'm concerned and I don't have shit to say to her.

"I'm yo momma, without me, you wouldn't have any of this," Alice said, pointing around.

"Get the fuck off my property and don't ever put your hands on Ahmina again." I said and walked into my home slamming the door in her face.

I didn't raise my voice, I didn't need too. She knew that she wasn't welcome here. Coming here she knew wasn't a good idea. What's more important to me right now is where the fuck is Quaneisha and how she didn't hear Alice jumping on Ahmina.

When I walked into the living room, Mina was still crying and Hope was standing in front of her telling her not to cry. Quaneisha was on her phone, texting somebody. This is my last day fucking with this bitch!

"Quan, what are doing? You didn't hear anything going on?" I asked.

"Yea, but I didn't want to get involved."

"Let me holla at you for a second."

I walked out of the white room, where we were at that nobody was supposed to be in. They seem to be in here more and more every day. Quan was getting the fuck out. This is the final straw. What the fuck do you mean you don't want to be involved? My sister is screaming and hollering and you don't think you need to check and make sure she is okay. I stood in front the foyer, while Quan took her time getting there.

"Quaneisha, this isn't working out. You can go on head do you baby."

"What do you mean? You don't want me in your family business so I was supposed to jump in Mina's business?"

"This is not just about that, we aren't getting anywhere. We are in the same place that we were when we first started fucking with each other. You are very aware of how I feel about my family. You go to the mall, nail shop with Mina and tell her all yo fucking problems but you hear her screaming and are not concerned?"

"I'm sorry. What do I need to do to make things right? What even happened? Why is she crying?"

"Bye, Quaneisha. I wish you the best." I said, opening the door.

"Why are you doing this? I'm sorry. We can fix this."

I didn't even respond after a few more moments she knew that I wasn't trying to hear anything she had to say. She made her way out the door, with her head hanging low and crying in shit. I really don't give a fuck anymore. I shut the door behind her and went to check on Mina.

"How does she know where we live?" Mina asked as I walked back into the white room.

She used to me always having the answer so I know that she wanted an answer. I didn't fucking know but I was damn sure going to find out. Hope was sitting on the couch, fighting her sleep. I picked up Hope and she put her head on my shoulder and damn near fell asleep instantly.

"Mina, I don't know but she won't be back here, I promise. Okay?"

"What the fuck did she say to you? How did yall end up fighting?"

"She told me to let her in the house and I said, no."

I shook my head; I know my momma and Mina. So I know that as soon as Mina said no, Alice swung on her. I can't believe Quan though. You always talking that ride or die shit; that I don't be trying to hear. I want a woman to have a family with not a bitch to be in the streets with me. When it's time for you to ride and you do nothing. My phone was vibrating in my pocket; I looked at it and its Quaneisha. I should have left that bitch alone after a couple fucks!

* * *

"HOW THE FUCK does Alice know where you live K?" E asked.

"I don't fucking know," I said.

"Is Mina alright?" Gotti asked.

"Yea, she's good."

We were sitting at E's and I was trying to figure out who the fuck told Alice where I live? E wants to kill Quan, but that's not necessary I'm just not fucking with her. I have to go meet with Lady H in the morning.

"E, so can you not follow muthafucking instructions?" Envii screamed.

Envii is perfect for this nigga E. She is just as crazy as him and nobody else is going to put up with either one of them. Gotti was shaking his head while Envii was all in E's face.

"Envii now is not the time you fucking psychco! Give me a minute!"

"I don't give a fuck what time it is muthafucka now is the time that we are going to discuss this!"

Envii was moving her head from side to side and taking her index finger pointing it in E's face. This is nothing new all they do is argue that's why it doesn't bother me. When they met each other it started with an argument and they have been arguing ever since. I was over to let them know about Alice and Quan.

"So why the fuck is the bitch at the nail shop talking about you?" Envii screamed.

"Envii get yo fucking hand, out my face! I don't want to hear no shit about a bitch right now!"

"You are not going to be happy until you wake up dead," Envii said and walked away.

"I'm getting a fucking divorce, I don't have to live like this," E said.

Gotti and I both started laughing. This nigga ain't going any damn where but every week he swears he is. We finished discussing business and what our next moves needed to be in the streets.

KAI MORAE

"LET me run in here and I'll be right back," D said.

I was ready for us to get into an argument, so he could go missing for a few days. I'm sick of looking at him. When I get out of work and school I have to look at him. I need a fucking break away from him. I saw Memphis's truck up the street I just hoped when Deontae came out the house that he didn't notice him. It was going to be some shit. Soon as that thought crossed Deontae came out the house.

I was driving, so I was ready to get rid of Deontae. I didn't give a fuck where he went. I just needed some space. D got in the car with a million plans. Little did he know he would be on a solo mission, on his two feet.

"I got stuff to do, I can't do all that right now," I said.

"So what's up Kai, you ready for a real nigga yet?" Memphis asked as he pulled up beside us.

I just sat back and didn't say anything. Deontae started going the fuck off "Nigga really, don't ever in yo life say nothing to my girl again!" I knew that shit was about to get worse, I could just feel it. "You need a real, nigga Kai, this nigga can't do anything for you. He riding around in yo car all day, while you work and he still ain't got no money." I mean Memphis did have a valid point, but Deontae's skin was turning red and he was embarrassed and mad as hell. I was looking at Deontae, waiting for him to say something.

"Bitch nigga, so what's up what are you trying to do?" Deontae said.

I turned my head to look at Memphis and he pulled out his gun pointing in my direction. If this muthafucka shoots he going to hit me first and I turned to look over at Deontae waiting for him to do something and I got nothing. This nigga takes a gun to Seven Eleven, but today no gun today. Deontae was still yelling and cussing at Memphis but I was going to be hit. I didn't have time for this shit. I sped the fuck off, if Memphis punk ass wanted to shoot, he would have all that fucking time. Some niggas just want to show their gun but won't shoot it. I had to get away from this nothing ass nigga.

* * *

ONCE I GOT home and replayed the situation that happened. I decided that I can't keep doing this dumb shit with D. He was just a dumb ass nigga and I deserved better than this dumb ass, silly bullshit. I needed to focus on me and keep my life in order. My phone is ringing and it's my cousin, I'm really not trying to go back out tonight.

"Hello," I said.

"Shod's locked up," Deena said.

It's always fucking something. Who has time to deal with this shit? Shod and I are closer than I am with anybody in my family. Are mothers use to be friends, that how my mom and dad met each other. Deena, on the other hand, I don't deal with. We communicate when we have to like right now. She's shod sister and she is a fucking rat ass bitch. She started complaining about the shit that was going wrong in her life like I could possibly be of some assistance. She must have forgotten who she was talking too.

"Let, me call you right back," I said, and before she could respond I hung the fuck up.

It wasn't shit that was going to be able to be done tonight about Shod so I would deal with it in the morning before I went to work because looking to Deena or his other sister for assistance was going to be a waste of everybody's time. Let alone. His momma Wanda, I'm sure she has taken whatever he had and has it in a slot machine with her. Deontae was calling, but I would be keeping my distance from him. I needed to take my ass to sleep so I could deal with Shod's business.

KURUPT

"HOW'S THE FAMILY?"LADY Heroine asked.

"Hope's good. Mina getting just started college. How is yours?"

"That's good, mine ain't shit but a fucking headache. Every day it's something with one of them muthafuckas."

Lady H is beautiful, but she is the craziest person I know. She's a BBW, light skin, long black hair that touches her ass, big brown eyes. Lady Heroine approached me after I took over Fat Ricky's block. Everybody knows Lady H, but if it's very few people she'll let sit at her table. Most niggas grow up idolizing the dope man, but I wanted to be like Lady Heroine. I use to hear stories about how crazy she was, but when I saw it with my own eyes I knew she wasn't the one to be fucked with.

"While you were gone it was kind of quiet. It's time to make some muthafucking noise," Lady H said.

I shook my head. If it's up to her anybody that isn't on our side will end up in a casket. She respects the way I handle my business on my side but if she hears that bodies are dropping that makes her day.

"On it."

"Hold on one second K."

"What the fuck is the problem now? I'm starting to believe all three of y'all muthafuckas are the dumbest niggas in the world!" Lady H screamed into her phone.

Everybody in the damn restaurant turned to look at us.

"It's best you muthafuckas mind y'all muthafucking business!" Lady Heroine screamed, the white lady sitting across from us damn near jumped out her seat.

I'm used to it and I know she ain't just a muthafucka that good. She's put in plenty of work.

"Let the dumb muthafucka sit there for a few days. If you think about going to get him, you'll regret it for the rest of yo muthafucking life Tyreek!" Lady H Screamed and threw her phone in her purse.

"Back to what I was saying. Is E, Alright?" Lady H asked.

"He good, he been out there fucking niggas up. With the day coming up he... Well, you know."

With the day E's mom died coming up we all already know how he's going to deal with it. It's going to be niggas dropping if they look at him wrong. He hasn't ever gotten over his mom's death and she passed over ten years ago.

"I got something I need you to handle for me," Lady H said.

"Whatever you need."

Lady H let me know what she needed to be done and I texted Bad News letting him know what I needed to get the job done. Lady H hardly ever asks for anything extra but considering this situation she needed someone else to handle it.

"Give a second, I gotta take this," I said as I got up.

Re-Re was calling. She is my mom's sister. When Alice put me out, Re-Re wanted me to stay with her but I didn't want too. I was so damn mad at the world; I didn't want to have to answer to anybody, so it was best that I stayed on my own. We always kept in touch.

"What's going on Re-Re?"

"We need to talk about Alice."

Re-Re and I have never discussed my mom and there was no need for us to start now. I still didn't have shit to say to her. Re- Re being the person she is, she wants to see the good in people and nothing else matters. I, on the other hand, wasn't trying to hear that shit in this situation.

"What's up auntie?"

"She needs some help baby and I know what she did to you and she was wrong, but she is still your mom."

"I'll pay for her to go to rehab."

That's all the fuck I was offering because any moral support was going to have to come from somewhere else. I don't have time for anything else right now especially for her. I got more important things that need my attention, like Hope and Mina. Where the fuck is her nigga at?

"She wants, to talk to you and Ahmina and she wants to get help, but I think that it would make it easier if you and Mina —"

"Re-Re I don't mean to cut you off but it's not going to happen. I'll call you when I get home."

"Alright, just think about it."

Wasn't shit to think about, the answer was no and I don't give a damn what nobody had to say even Re-Re. I made my way back to the restaurant to finish up this business, so I could get home with no intentions of calling Re-Re back.

KAI MORAE

"What's up Kai Morae?" Shod said, once the phones connected.

"What's up?"

Between his momma and his sisters they were all getting on my damn nerves and I'm ready for him to get the fuck out here. His momma hates me and she has all my life. I don't know why and at this point it really doesn't matter. For whatever reason, she thinks she needs to call me every day. Just like I already knew everything that Shod had at her house was gone.

I fuck with Shod only when it comes to my business in the streets. So fucking with somebody else was out the question. The way that it is looking he isn't coming home any time soon. He's going to be sitting down, for at least a year. He trying to tell me to get with his best friend, but that ain't going to work. I'm agreeing with everything that he's saying but I have to figure something else out. All I got is what Shod had at his mom's and what he had just given me before he got pulled over.

We finished up the visit and I told him I was going to get with his people but that wasn't happening. Darin is his friend, not mines and I don't trust him. The list of people that I trust is really short and I'm not taking any chances right now. I needed to figure out what the fuck I was going to do when everything was all gone. I headed over to Alice's; so I could make my way to work.

I was still ignoring Deontae; I didn't have shit to say to him. The problems that I have he can't be of any assistance, so it's really no reason for us to talk. I didn't have time to talk to Alice today, so this would be really quick and fast, I'm already going to be late to work.

"Hey, what's going on Kai Morae?" Alice said as I walked into her home.

Alice kept a very clean home and her furniture and television are newer than mine. She has pictures of a little boy and girl, throughout the house but I don't know who they are. From their outfits, the pictures are old. She's always saying she doesn't have anybody since Bruce died. She always in my damn business trying to give me relationship advice; I want to know who these kids in this picture are.

"Alice, who is this little boy and girl?"

"Where yo broke ass boyfriend at?"

All I could do was laugh because she was right that nigga is broke as hell. I handed Alice what she requested and she gave me money. I guess that was her way of telling me none of my damn business. She'd know before I did where broke ass Deontae is. Before Alice started talking about the news and what's going wrong in the world today. I got a piece of candy out of the candy jar on the end table and took my ass to work.

* * *

"Katrina, hurry the fuck up so I can go home!" I screamed into the phone and hung up.

I didn't feel like even being here to pick her ass up and now she's talking all day long. An old two-door truck pulled up on the opposite side of the street. I was waiting for Katrina to come out of Sara's. Deontae was walking to Sara's. I would have rather him not seen me, but with this car, he knows it's me. I really don't give a fuck.

"I hope you really leave his broke ass alone, he called over here trying to negotiate the price of a t-shirt," Katrina said, as she got in the car.

I just shook my head. So where getting customers to give you the full amount, taking the extra few dollars pocketing it and doing what with it buying some candy from the corner store. Considering the fact that it's already a drought ain't too much negotiating going to get you. Not dealing with him and his family has been a weight lifted off my shoulders. I heard, Katrina dogging Deontae, down to his socks but I just didn't know what else I was going to do. Deontae was convenient and shit I get lonely sometimes. Nobody else was checking for me.

KURUPT

"RE-RE, what is that you are asking me to do? Go sit with her in some meetings or something?" I asked.

"I know that she did wrong in the past but I think it will help the both of you heal if you give her a second chance," Re-Re said.

I had just got to Re-Re's and I was already ready to go. I came here to give her the information, for the rehab that I paid for Alice to go to. That was it and if Re-Re's support wasn't enough then I didn't know what to tell her. Hope, was watching something on her I-pad, sitting next to me. I know that she was getting sleepy so we won't be here long. I needed to go get Mina and go home.

"What's changed why does she want to talk to us all of a sudden?"

"She starting using, once Bruce died and I think that she has hit rock bottom and she's at the point she wants to right her wrongs."

So popping up at my house and jumping on Mina was a great fucking start. I still wanted to know how the fuck she knows where I live. I've hired a security company to watch my house and Ahmina at all times. I didn't tell Ahmina because I can hear her fucking mouth and this has been done to protect her not to be in her business. She doesn't go anywhere but the mall, nail shop or Gotti's any damn way. Somebody was knocking on Re-Re door, so she got up to get it.

I started playing with Hope and looked up Alice was staring in my face. Re-Re didn't know I was coming so either, Alice stalking me or it's a coincidence. I was going to listen to whatever she had to say because I didn't have shit to say.

"Let me take Hope in the other room, while yall talk," Re-Re said, picking up Hope.

"You're doing a good job, with Hope. Better than that hoe Quita would have done."

"Thanks."

I picked up the remote and flipped through a few channels. My momma wasn't saying anything she was just staring at me. Even with as much as I hated her for so many years, I still don't like to see her like this. I would never have thought my momma would be on drugs. Yes, I sell drugs and somebody else's momma is probably using my drugs right now but I just never thought it would be mine.

"I'm sorry Kamal. I was wrong and I shouldn't have put you out. I should have put you and Ahmina first." Alice said, looking away from me.

I wasn't responding to that. I would never put anything before Hope, shit Ahmina and she's my sister. I will never be able to understand why she made the decision she did. I don't hate her, but I also don't trust her either.

"You ready to get some help?"

"Who told you my business, nosey ass Re-Re?"

"Fuck you bitch, I ain't nosey!" Re-Re yelled from the other room.

I had to talk to Ahmina about talking to Alice. After Alice kicked her ass; I don't know what she's going to say. When she was younger she would say that she wanted to see her all the time. As she got older she stopped and until Alice showed up at the house we haven't talked about Alice, in years.

"I got one question doe. How do you know where I live?"

"That hoe Quan; I'm glad you left her alone and yea I'm ready to get some help."

I talked to Alice for about an hour and we agreed to meet here in the morning to check-in to rehab. I think that it will just be Re-Re and I going with her, but I'm going to try to talk to Ahmina. I'm going to do this, but I'm going to have to keep Alice at a distance until I know that she is going to do the right thing. After I get Mina and take her and Hope home I'm going to see Quan. I don't give a fuck who it is? You don't talk outside of my home to any muthafucking body!

* * *

WHEN I GOT to Quan's there was an eviction notice on the front door. I knocked on the door and it opened. It was empty from what I saw, so there was no reason for me to go in. I called Quan, but she didn't answer that bitch had been calling and texting me non-stop but now she doesn't want to talk all of a sudden. I'll run into her soon.

QUANEISHA

"I TOLD YOU, I don't know where his spots are at. I never went with him to do his business," I said for the hundredth time.

"What did his momma tell you?" Red asked.

"She didn't get past the front door, she doesn't know anything."

As those words left my mouth Ray-Ray walked by through the dining room in a t-shirt and panties. I wish he would send this bitch back where he found her. I am really getting sick of her ass. A while ago my man Red put this plan together for me to get with Kurupt, but when he caught a case, that threw a wrench into our plans. As time went by I caught feelings for Kamal and I was just waiting for him to choose me and make me his girlfriend so I could get out of this hood ass Polygamy situation with Ray-Ray and Red. He doesn't have enough dick for me let alone Ray-Ray. She needs to go home and raise her, son what type of mother is she?

"I'm going to need to run to the springs tomorrow," Ray-Ray said.

I know she had to be talking to Red because the bitch can't ride with me to seven eleven, so an hour ride to Colorado Springs wasn't going to happen. The broke bitch needed to get a car and a fucking job because she'd be eating air fucking around with Red and I. I rolled my eyes and got up and went to take a bath. I wanted to get mine since I couldn't guarantee to get one from Red. I had get mine for myself while thinking about Kurupt definitely not Red's ass.

I grabbed my phone, it was Kurupt asking me where did I live, he wanted to see me. I knew he would come back. I knew he really cared about me too. He was just in his feeling about Alice. I knew that Alice was Kurupt's mom because she told everybody in the hood that was her son. It saved her ass a few times because niggas already know that fucking with her it was a chance that you would end up missing.

Kurupt is really private, so he told me that he didn't talk to his mom but he didn't tell me anything else. The only reason why I know Kamal's middle name is because they said it in court a few times that I went. We've been kicking it for a while now and we haven't spent one holiday together or each other's birthdays. He's bought me a few things and gave me money a few times but I think that's just out of habit. That nigga damn near treated me like the people outside the gas station asking for change. I've seen him give them all the dollar bills in his pocket, which was damn near a stack. **Lunch tomorrow, meet me at noon at Benihana's**, Kurupt texted me.

I'm spinning Red dumb ass from this point on and I'm going to get Kurupt to be my man. **I'll be there in a red dress, with no panties**. I texted back, he texted me back the tongue and water emoji. I got him!

KAI MORAE

AFTER A FEW DRINKS, I found myself, calling Deontae. I need to get some more niggas to call, I thought to myself as I got up, to get something to drink. I had just finished up my homework and am waiting for Deontae to get here. I had a text from Katrina, **Let's go shopping tomorrow**. I need a break so that sounded like a plan. It had been a few hours since I talked to Deontae, so it looked like he wasn't coming. I wasn't calling and begging his broke ass to come see me. I just took my ass to sleep.

* * *

"I'M HUNGRY, let's go to Waffle House," Katrina said.

We had just left out of the mall and I was ready to go home we had been out all day. She was driving, so I guess we were going. Gina was calling me, but I wasn't in the mood to deal with them today. I woke up this morning to miss calls from Deontae, but I didn't even bother calling him back. I was sober and back to fucking reality. I listened to Gina's voicemail she left and she said that Deontae was locked up. I deleted the message and scrolled my Facebook timeline.

It was packed when we pulled up. At what time, it is I'm not surprised. Katrina was checking her makeup, as I got out the car. I was getting calls, from the jail I thought it might be Shod, so I answered as soon as I heard that it was Deontae I just hung up.

"What's up Kai, how are you doing?" I heard, a man say.

I turned around it was the man from the mall, nail shop and Metro. I started walking behind Katrina into the restaurant. Katrina was talking to me but I wasn't listening I was thinking about the nigga a standing behind me in line.

"Damn, why do you have to be so mean?" Kamal asked.

"Wassup, Kurupt? Toni said while shaking up with Kamal but looking at me shaking his head.

Toni has been a bitch and I have never liked him, he needs to be worried about the bitch that's playing him for diapers and Similac for a baby that's not even his. What I do is nobody's concern but mine. As far as I am concerned I'm single and if Toni runs his mouth like I know he will I will finally be set free for good.

"I'm not mean, I just don't know you," I said.

"Well, I've been trying to get to know you and you won't give me a chance," Kamal said.

It was our time to order, so Katrina and I made our way up to the counter. A part of me wanted to give somebody else a chance. Why does Kamal want to talk to me? He is fine as hell and can have any bitch he keeps trying to talk to me. He wants something, or it's some bullshit involved. What would he want with my big ass?

We ordered our food and Kamal came and sat by Katrina and I. Katrina was hitting my arm, all she sees is dollar signs with any nigga and that's why she's so concerned. If I get something extra, she might be able to get a few more dollars here and there. My phone was vibrating it was a Facebook message from Toni; you know I'm telling, right? I honestly didn't give a fuck who he told. Deontae wasn't for me he is for everybody and he is in jail again is my opportunity to see what else is out here. I don't know shit about Kamal and I'm going to have to do a real live investigation, but I got some time. I wouldn't be getting Deontae out of jail and if left up to his family that nigga is there.

"Mina, you already know what I want, just order," Kamal said.

The little girl I saw him with at school, ran up to where we were sitting. She is the prettiest chocolate baby I have ever seen. Katrina was acknowledging how pretty she is. Before Kamal could respond, the baby told Katrina "Thank you." We were waiting, for our food to come out.

"That's your daughter?" I asked.

"Yes, my baby Hope."

Hope was standing in front of Katrina and me, telling us hi. I wanted to ask where her momma was, but I didn't want to be nosy. Kamal smelled, so good and the way he handled himself I knew that he was older than me but he didn't look it.

"You going to give me a chance, I don't have a baby momma if that's what your excuse was going to be," Kamal said.

"She still, doesn't want you, let it go. I'm Mina, K's sister." Mina said as she walked up to us.

Katrina went to get our food and I couldn't help but laugh. Something was telling me not to do it but it damn sure wasn't Toni's threat. Fuck it I thought, as I took Kamal's phone out of his hand and put my number in it and gave it back to him. I got up out of my seat and made my way out the door, with Katrina.

"Is, this a fake number? I'm about to call it right now?" I heard Kamal say from behind me.

Then a number I didn't know popped up, it was Kamal. I answered it and just laughed. "Had to check before you left the parking lot, I'm going to call you later," Kamal said. "I wouldn't have given you a fake number, but okay," I said and hung up. Katrina was more excited than I was. She turned, down the music so I knew her talk a lot ass was about to get started talking.

"Bitch, did you see his watch and how the bitches and niggas were all staring at him. He's that nigga for sure Fuck Deontae broke ass! You need to get with him," Katrina said.

I wasn't thinking about that niggas watch or the bitches or niggas that was looking at him. Her being focused on that hasn't got her anywhere yet. I'm not looking for a nigga to save me. Her and every other female that I know that is waiting to be saved that's not who I am and I'm not willing to turn into that bitch for no nigga.

48

KURUPT

J put up three fingers and as I dropped the last one Gotti kicked in the front door. This nigga Red was acting like a bitch and sending niggas in my traps so it was a must that he knew that this would not be tolerated. I had got the word, from Lady H; Red was at his baby momma's house cooking up my shit that he took. It was two clown cars outside, so at least those niggas were in here. I'm not hurting, nobody kids. Women can live too as long as they fully understand that talking outside this house they would end up being buried by their nigga.

Gotti led the way through the house; they were clearly high because nobody had come out when the door smacked the ground with a loud ass thump. The music was loud throughout the house but it wasn't that damn loud. I wanted Red, not Devin or Smoke, but they were who were in the kitchen. Gotti and Enforcer were making their rounds around the house. Devin and Smoke's backs were facing me. I turned the volume down on whosever phone was playing the music on the counter. Devin and Smoke both turned around at the same damn time. Gotti and E were standing in the doorway, without Red so these niggas were going to have to go for the boss. Never be an underpaid worker, by a nigga playing boss with somebody else shit.

"You can have everything," Devin said.

"It's mine, so how kind of you to offer me what you haven't put up your nose," I said.

"Where the fuck is Red?" Gotti asked.

The room got quiet nobody wanted to talk all of a sudden. They had opened one of the keys, but the others were still in the plastic untouched. E was putting, them into the bag they came out of when they were taken. Once he finished, he took his AR15 and hit it across Devin's face. His patience is very thin. Devin fell to the ground swiftly. Smoke threw up his hands, to show that he was ready to surrender.

"He's with Ray-Ray, she lives in the Springs–" Smoke said before Gotti shot him.

I walked over to where Devin was laid on the ground clutching his head. I pulled, out my PPS and let off few rounds, into Devin's torso and then the final one into his skull. We made our way out the kitchen. Gotti had brought red baby momma Diamond, to the living room. She was smoking a cigarette. She used to this, shit fucking with broke ass Red.

"I didn't see anything," Diamond said, as we walked through the living room.

That was all I needed to know, if anything else was to transpire she would be the first to go before Red. As soon as I find out where exactly Red is his ass is got. I don't have time to keep playing with these niggas I have to get them before they get me. I have a daughter to raise.

"Who the fuck has an empty safe? Diamond said it was for show," E said laughing.

That shit didn't surprise me. Red is a clown and if I wouldn't have found out that he was responsible for taking my shit then he would have just fucked up the dope and not have had shit at the end. This nigga has had a problem with me forever but I don't know why and neither the fuck do I care. I never did anything to that bitch ass nigga! It's enough money out here for everybody to eat, but when you're broke and envious of the next nigga you'll never get anywhere.

"Alright, I'll see yall tomorrow," I said, as I got into my truck.

* * *

WHEN I WOKE UP, Yellow was on my mind so I had to call her. It wasn't Hope or Mina, the streets or money for a change. I don't know what it is about her. We have been on the phone for over two hours, and I ain't sick of her yet. I have a short attention span and I don't even like talking on the phone.

"What are you going to school for?" I asked.

"Criminal Justice—"

"Damn, you the police like Mina."

We both laughed. I didn't want to get up but I got a lot of shit to do today. I needed to go to the springs and make sure Alice's; house is packed up so her stuff could be shipped back up here. She needed to get the fuck away from there. She not coming to my house, but she doesn't need to be there either. I needed to get up and get dressed because Hope would be up soon.

"I gotta come yo way today. You want to get something to eat later?" I asked.

"Yea, we can."

From the time that we have talked I learned that she had a broke ass ex-boyfriend. Once she gave me her number they were over. He was just a broke ass nigga that was using her and didn't know what he had. She didn't come right out and say it but I'm a man and that's what it is. He'll be woken up soon. I know that she doesn't believe that I don't fuck with Quita. It's hard for a lot of people to believe but bitches are deadbeats too, they just don't get talked about as much.

"K, I need some money!" Mina screamed, from the other side of my bedroom door.

"Mina, get a job!"

Yellow, was at work now she had to go. I didn't want her to hang up. I told, her I would see her in a minute before I disconnected the call. I got up and threw on some basketball shorts and a shirt. Mina was now banging on the door.

"Cuz did you hear me say get a job?" I asked as I walked around Mina.

I walked down the hall to Hope's room she was standing up in her crib. As I walked into the room, a smile spread across her face. She reminded me so much of what Alice use to look like. Mina was on my heels. Every other day, she needs money and she comes asking already knowing where money is for her to just get it. We made our way down the stairs. I put Hope in her chair and started to make breakfast.

"Mina, for the last time, get it out that cookie jar," I said.

"Do, I have to go with you to see momma?" Mina asked.

I figured this was coming, I know that she really didn't want to go. We had talked about it a few times and when she told me she would go I knew it was just so I would shut the fuck up and quit talking to her. If nobody else doesn't understand how she feels, I do shit I been the one here with Mina this whole time. I just want her to give it a chance. I never thought I would even consider seeing Alice again, let alone, talking to her but if I can so can Mina black ass.

"You are going, you already said you would."

"Alright, I'll go but I need a new bag," Mina said.

"We can go shopping, tomorrow, I need you to watch Hope after we go see momma. I got a date."

KAI MORAE

IN THE FEW days I've been talking to Kamal I been a great mood. I wake up happy as hell. When he calls me he asks me how I'm doing. He's not calling wanting something from me. Kamal has been such a breath of fresh air. I'm not getting caught up in any shit; I'm just going to enjoy this while it lasts. I'm sure this isn't something that's going to last long. The type of nigga he is I'm sure he'll be on to the next soon.

I have been ignoring Gina and everybody else that is affiliated with Deontae. I opened my desk to check my phone I had a message from Kamal; I hope you're having a good day at work. Little things like that make such a big difference if it was Deontae he would have texted, I'm going to come get yo car on yo lunch or can run me here or there. These customers are getting on my nerves and I'm just ready to go home and get ready to see Kamal. The only thing, that's making me second guess him is his missing baby momma. Shit until I'm shown different I'm going to try to put aside and see what he's all about. I don't have shit to lose.

* * *

"I got it," Kamal said, as he opened the door for me to get in his truck.

TWENTY YEARS OLD, and never had been on a date before tonight. I was nervous, while I was getting ready, but I had a few shots and smoked a black so I was feeling alright now. I decided to put on a black fitted dress and knee-high boots. Kamal was looking good as fuck and smelling like Givenchy.

"How was work?"

"It was alright, I'm glad I don't have to go back until Monday," I said.

Kamal hasn't told me that he was a hustla, but I could tell by the way he moved, walked and talked. I felt so comfortable like I knew him for longer than I have. I don't think I've laughed or smiled as much as I have since I've been talking to him in a long time. We have talked about everything, except our parents. I loved how close he and Mina are. Also how much he loves is daughter, he talks about her so much and looking at him right now as he talks about Hope; he means what he is saying.

"Tell me about your people, yo mom, and pops," Kamal said.

I took a deep breath and rolled my eyes as thoughts of my mom came in, "well my mom and I don't have a relationship."

"Sounds like my mom, I've been on my own since I was sixteen, it's still hope for you and yo mom doe. I just got back in touch with her after some years."

I heard him and maybe in fairytale land, there was a chance and that's good for him and his mom. I'm not trying to workout shit with my mom. She has never fucked with me her whole life and we can keep it like it is as far as I'm concerned. As we drove up the highway, I

53

was able to clear my head and the more we conversed the better I got to Kamal the more I really liked him. As Jagged Edge "Lace you" came out the speakers, I started to get sleepy.

KURUPT

"WHAT YOU KNOW ABOUT THIS?" I asked, as Anita Baker's "Caught Up in the Rapture", came on.

I looked over and yellow had fallen asleep on me and must have been tired as hell she was snoring. As I pulled into the parking lot of the Cheesecake Factory, I didn't want to wake her up. She is knocked the fuck out.

"Yellow, Yellow."

She started to wake up. She is really beautiful and was refreshing to meets someone that doesn't know who you are and wants nothing from you. We both need this and I'm not letting up. Even when her ass has an attitude or get smart; I'm not going anywhere. She didn't say anything about her dad so either he's dead, locked up or she doesn't know who he is. I wasn't about to ask again; maybe it's a sensitive subject.

"How long was I sleep?"

"Not long."

I got out the car, to get her door. I'm starving and Yellow clearly needs to get to bed soon. Quaneisha was blowing up my phone. Trying to get to my house because she was homeless back with her momma it wasn't going to happen. We would be moving soon as I find something because there is a chance too many people know where I live. I told her we will have to see about us only so I can keep her arm's length so I know what the fuck she might be doing. After I cussed her out about discussing my address with anybody; she tried to play dumb like she didn't know what I was talking about. Alice is guilty of being a lot of things a liar isn't one of them. I'll never fuck with Quan again like that. Yellow, kept looking at her phone, "yo ex-calling?" I asked.

"Naw his momma."

I'm glad she was honest. Nothing is worse than a lying ass bitch. We ordered our food and Yellow, ran to the bathroom. I felt somebody tap me on the shoulder and it was Quan. Broke bitches, do the most splurging on shit they can't afford; so I'm not surprised.

"Who the fuck is that?" Quan asked, damn near screaming.

"None of yo fucking business and lower yo fucking voice when you talking to me."

Her rat ass friend Ray-Ray started laughing and Quan was embarrassed didn't say shit else just stormed off. I didn't give a fuck how mad she was. Quaneisha was never my bitch and there was never any confusion before about that so there's none now.

Shortly after Quan stormed off, Yellow came back to the table. I'm glad she missed that shit because this would be over before it started. A white lady in the booth across from us was still staring at me. I stuck up my middle finger and the bitch finally looked away.

"Um, why are you tripping with that lady?" Yellow asked.

"Yellow, cuz she was staring at me all in my face."

We laughed; Yellow was cheesing and shaking her head. Shit, I can't remember the last time I've been on a date. We picked up talking where we left off. I'm really feeling Yellow and the way she smiling and looking at me, I know the feeling is mutual.

"You always at work, what else do you be doing?"

"Nothing, if I'm not I'm not with my friends I'm at home."

Kai is just too good to be true. The only issue I got is how she talks down about herself. I can't deal with that shit. "So what is it? Why you wanna get to know my big ass?" I don't even know how to respond to that. I know that some people are insecure, but I wasn't expecting that.

"Kai, I love the way you look and I don't want anything from you."

Kai was embarrassed and didn't know what to say. I can tell that's something that she's never heard. She got all these dreams but she doubts herself and clearly has issues with the way she looks. I don't know if that old nigga got her like this, or this is the way she's always been. I know some niggas can break you down bad but I'm not that nigga. We finished up our food and made our way back to Yellows. Yellow was quiet most of the way.

"What are you doing tomorrow?" I asked, as pulled up back to Yellow's apartment.

"I need to study and other than that nothing much."

"Well I'll let you study tomorrow but Sunday, you should come over. So you can get to know Hope and Mina."

"I would like to do that."

Yellow was biting her nail which I noticed she did when she was nervous. I got out so that I could walk her to her building.

"Thank you, for dinner. I enjoyed myself tonight," I said.

"I should be telling you to thank you. Thanks, I enjoyed myself too. Be careful and Call me when you get home." Yellow said as she walked to her door.

Whether yellow liked it or not which what I planned for her she was going to love it and be my woman soon. I just had to see what Hope and Mina thought about her. I'm going to have Gotti and E come through too because if they know her or heard of Yellow it's a not going to happen. I made my way to the highway as I lit my blunt. Keith Sweat, "I'll Give all my Love To you" was coming through my speakers.

Quan's name popped up on my dashboard. I was going to end this, shit right now. She is fully aware of who I am and what I am not going to allow. She tried it because she was in her feelings and then Ray-Ray was with her. What I will not do is argue with no bitch about nothing. No bitch is excluded from that. If you can't talk to me like you got some fucking sense than we won't talk.

"What's up Quan?"

"So, that's what you are doing now? Taking bitches to dinner! I've been fucking with you for how long and the other day was the first time you ever took me anywhere!"

The only reason why I took her out then was that she's not welcome back in my home and she's homeless. She was in my ear crying and screaming, but I didn't want to hear that shit. Where the fuck was her antennas when Alice was jumping on Mina? We have been headed nowhere for too long, she needs to just move on with her life and let it go.

"It doesn't matter Quaneisha, but if you keep yelling my fucking ear I'm going to hang up."

"We are not done, you just can't fuck with one day and then boom just like that fucking with that fat ass bi–"

I hung up on her ass before she could finish her sentence. She'll go fuck with another nigga that has a bag and get the same thing that I gave her nothing. A few dollars and she feels like the baddest bitch in the city but still remain in the same position she was when she met them. I was going to have to find a new place ASAP that's the only thing that Quaneisha knows about me is where I live. I never told her anything because we were never serious and I knew that it was always temporary. I called Yellow, as I made my way home.

* * *

LADY H WANTED me to take care of a problem she was having with Samantha who was responsible for cleaning her money for her. With her not playing her position it could put Lady H and her entire organization is a compromising position. Lady H is a lot like E she gets the job done but she's not quietly. That's why she requested that I handle Sam.

As I sat a few tables away from Samantha at Denver's Biscuit Company. I had small talk with Brionna who is Bad News wife. To the people in the restaurant, she's just a nice looking well-dressed white woman enjoying breakfast. What none of them know is that she is one of the best thieves' I know besides Envii; she just too damn loud to use for this. That was exactly what I needed everybody to think including Samantha who was enjoying her shrimp and grits the only thing she didn't know was that would be her last meal. She missed Brionna going into her purse taking her keys. Shit, to be honest, it happened so fast I missed it too.

Sam was flagging down the waitress to pay her bill, so I placed some money on the table and made my way out of the restaurant.

As I hit the fob on 2010, Ford Focus I was driving that is parked three cars away from Sam's car. I knew that Samantha would be here because she eats breakfast here every Tuesday. Sam made her way to her car while looking through her purse for her keys. Unbeknownst to her are in my pocket, Brionna was walking over to get to offer her help. Samantha's phone is in my other pocket powered off. Once Sam accepted Brionna's help, I pulled off and made my way to Sam's home.

* * *

I STOOD in Samantha's foyer waiting for her to come through the door Brionna texted me they were coming around the corner. Brionna was following her a few cars behind. I had cut the wires to the camera last night and Samantha clueless ass hadn't noticed. I texted Shelly who works with ADT and her security system were disable early this morning. Soon as I heard the key in the lock I secured the silencer in my on my gun. Samantha didn't notice me behind the door. Lady Heroine wanted her shot in her back twenty-three times for the twenty-three thousand she had stolen and her tongue because she had given Lady Heroine her word and didn't keep it. She also wanted her phone but didn't tell me why. With the first shot to the head, Samantha instantly smacked her hardwood floor. I had to be sure that all twenty-three shots were done because Lady H is very critical and if that's what she asks for then that is what she wants to be done.

I finished my task at hand and made my way out to get rid of this Focus. As I pulled up to The Shop I hit a button to let me into the back and then hopped out and handed the keys to my man Desean. So he can get rid of the car. I have an auto repair, custom paint shop. I love cars and with this business it comes in handy when I need to get rid of them as well. Only my people use and are aware of the chop shop in the back. I checked in with the manager that runs my shop to make sure everything is running smoothly and made way out. Now I have to get this bitch tongue to Lady H before she leaves town.

KAI MORAE

"*B*itch, why didn't you bring me to Sunday dinner with you?" Katrina Yelled, into the phone.

"Bitch, you weren't invited. I don't even know where this is going. I'm not going to invite nobody to his house," I said.

I was sitting in front of Kamal's house. Deontae only came to my mind, when I wasn't around Kamal or on the phone with him which wasn't very often. A part of me felt guilty because I have been loyal to Deontae for so long and I feel as if I'm wrong for even entertaining Kamal. Then I have Katrina yelling at me regularly telling me fuck Deontae.

"I hope you really, leave Deontae alone and fuck with ol boy. Deontae can't do anything for you but tear you back down. "Girl I saw Nique on Facebook, talking about that was her man. So fuck him for real, for real!"

"Alright bitch I have to go, I been sitting out in front of this his house for too damn long!"

I hung up on Katrina; this was nothing new it was always some bitch that swears their his bitch. Far as I was concerned they could buy Ramon noodles, phone cards and make that trip to go see them because as long as Kamal stayed acting right I have no intentions of fucking with Deontae again. I had finally returned Gina's calls and she told me that Deontae was going to take a plea and get up to ninety days. So Kamal has ninety days to step up and keep my attention.

"Mina was going to call the police. If you would have set outside any longer," Kamal said as he opened the door.

I laughed, I was out there a while and in this neighborhood, I'm surprised none of these white people didn't call the police on me. As I walked through his house, it was pictures of Mina and Hope all throughout the house. As we walked into the living room, Hope was sitting in the middle of the floor surrounded by toys.

"I thought you were lying when you said, she was coming over here," Mina said as she walked in the room.

"Shut up, Yellow this is Mina and Mina this is Kai," Kamal said.

We both said hi to each other. She is a really pretty girl; she looks familiar like I know her from somewhere. Mina is chocolate, with long black straight hair, big brown eyes like Kamal and thicker than a snicker. Kamal has invited me over to eat, but I don't even know if this nigga can even cook.

"You want something to drink or something?" Kamal asked.

"No, I'm good right now.

Then Gotti walked into the room, I wasn't expecting to see him. I don't personally know Gotti but Deontae was fucking with him, moving his shit for a minute. Hope jumped up and ran towards Gotti. I was hoping Gotti didn't remember who I was we only been around each other a few times.

"K really like you, he doesn't even lik–," Mina attempted to say before Kamal came back in the room.

"Gotti, this is Kai I was telling you about. Kai, this my man's Gotti." Kamal said.

Gotti reached out to shake my hand and the way he looked at me, he knew who I was. Deontae probably owes him some money. I didn't pay it any mind and just said, hi and focused my attention back to the TV. Whatever issue he had with Deontae, he was going to need to address that with him or with, the bitches that are claiming him today.

"Shut up, damn, please! I should have left yo ass at home!" I heard a man scream.

"Fuck you! I should have left you a long time ago and we wouldn't even have to have this conversation! You ain't shit! Ya daddy ain't shit! It's only one person in your family who is muthafucka!" A woman screamed.

Nobody had a concerned look on their face, so shit if they weren't worried neither was I. Kamal, had sat next to me and Mina was on the other side of me and Gotti, had left the room.

"Uncle E!" Hope screamed as she ran towards the man and woman that were still arguing back and forth with each other.

"You have to excuse, them they crazy as fuck both of em," Kamal said.

I laughed and shook my head. Kamal introduced me to Envii and Enforcer and they started right back arguing as soon as they both spoke to me. Enforcer is cute he has a caramel complexion neatly trimmed beard and goatee, curly black hair like he's mixed with something. He's tatted up and he works out from looking at him. Envii is really pretty caramel complexion, long black hair; she has a mole right below her nose that stands out. She's gorgeous but loud and as fuck!

They seemed to be a close-knit family. Kamal had told me about Gotti and Enforcer being his best friends since they were kids. Kamal and E left the room and Envii sat next to me, "Kurupt must like you I've never met anybody that he fucked with before." Envii said. I just smiled, I didn't know what to say, she could be just telling me anything or it could be the truth. Hope walked up to me reaching for me to pick her up.

"If Hope likes you, you in there," Envii said and Mina cosigned.

I loved kids, I always wanted a baby but I knew that it wouldn't be a good idea right now. I really wasn't paying any attention to the game that Mina and Envii were attempting to give me. I don't know either one of them but from dealing with bitches I know that it could be the truth, but it could also be some bullshit trying to gas me up.

It was just a breath of fresh air, being around new people. I was trying to relax and be open to getting to know them and not let my past prevent anything that may be coming in the future but it's going to easier said than done.

KURUPT

"YOU MUST LIKE KAI, you already inviting her to Sunday dinner," Gotti said while flipping over the chicken.

"She cool, I do like her. Do either one of you niggas know her?"

"Naw, I have never seen her before," E said.

"I don't know her like that, but I know she was fucking with broke ass Deontae. I gave him a phone, 6084 and that nigga didn't even know what to do with it." Gotti said.

"O, yea I know that," I said.

I was finishing up dinner so we could eat soon. Well Gotti and I that nigga E don't cook. That's not his thing or Envii's all they do is eat at restaurants. We tried to get together, on Sundays if time permitted. They are the only real family that I have outside of Mina and Hope. I've been trying to build shit back up with Alice, but she's not back in like that. Aunt Re-Re, doesn't come to my house and we talk regularly but that's it. I don't fuck with anybody outside of the people in this house. That is why it's important for me for Kai to meet them to see what they think about her and vice versa.

I went back into the living room to check on Kai before Envii talks her to death or scare the fuck away. I had tried to warn her about E and Envii, but shit you gotta see them to believe that people really act the way they do.

"Don't be getting on her fucking nerves, Envii with yo loud ass," I said and Kai turned around and smiled at me.

I was doing some shit that I very rarely did and going out of my way to make time and bring Kai into my world. I just hoped that she wasn't on any bullshit and didn't switch up on a nigga. Hope was sitting on her lap and not Mina's that surprised me. I didn't want to rush shit and move to fast, but niggas also ain't getting any younger to keep playing games. I'm twenty-seven now, ready to settle down and have somebody to come home to every night. By the way that Kai move, I can tell that she hesitating to move too fast. She also not about to play me for no broke ass little nigga either.

"Aye Kurupt, come here for a second," Gotti hollered from the kitchen.

E is pacing back and forth so, it must be some bullshit going on. Neither one of them were saying nothing. Gotti always plays it cool, even when he's mad you'll never know unless he told you. "I fucking told you to that I should have killed that bitch," E said.

"Calm, the fuck down. Word is that Quaneisha fucking with that nigga Red, Goddess just said she saw them together at Park Meadows." Gotti said, showing me a picture of Quaneisha, Red, and Ray-Ray.

I didn't say anything, I just sat there. When the clock strike midnight Quaneisha will be dead, there's nothing else that needs to be said. I could have let E kill her, but this was personal and I needed to handle this myself. As soon as family time is over, it will be time to send Quaneisha to the crossroads.

* * *

"You don't have to drive back home tonight," I said.

"I'm not staying here," Kai said.

"I didn't say let me get see yo panties. I took yo keys so yo can't go home anyway. Make yourself at home." I kissed Kai on her forehead and got Hope out of her lap, so I could get her ready for bed.

"Are you letting Kai stay here? After what happened with Quaneisha?" Mina asked, standing in the doorway of Hope's room.

"Yea, you don't want her to be here? We are moving Mina, so nobody is going to know where we live but us."

"I mean she's cool and I don't think she's like Quaneisha, but I was just asking. Do you really like her? Or are you just fucking with her for right now."

"Naw, I like her but stay out my damn business detective"

"Good night dad," Hope said as I laid her down.

"Good night baby."

I went back downstairs and Kai was still sitting on the couch. I sat down next to her and turned to Martin. She wasn't paying attention to the TV; she was too busy on her phone. I had texted Quan and told her to get a room and my phone was vibrating and like I figured it was her telling me the room number, but it was Gotti. Soon as Kai fall asleep, I was going to see that bitch!

"You can sleep in one of the guest rooms if you want because you can't sleep on my couch," I said, laughing but I meant that shit.

Kai rolled her eyes and hit me with one of the pillows. Sunday dinner was a success and she was able to handle E and Envii, shit so everything else should be a walk in the park from here on out. Hope really likes her and Mina must like her if not she would have been talking shit loud enough for her to hear downstairs.

"Kai!" Mina yelled.

Kai got up to go see what she wanted and I slapped her ass as she walked by; she just smiled. I didn't want to leave her, but I needed to handle Quan ASAP, she couldn't live too much longer.

KAI MORAE

THERE WAS A NOTE, on the pillow next to me. *I had to run out, for a minute to get a few things I'll be right back. You better not leave til I get back −K*

That was the best I've slept in months. I slept in Kamal's bed alone; if he would have slept with me I wouldn't have minded. I heard crying and I looked over at the baby monitor on the nightstand and went to check on Hope. Mina beat me to get her.

"I thought you were gone," Mina said.

"Naw, when K gets back I'm going to head home."

"K made breakfast, he should be right back."

I went to get myself together, so I could head downstairs. I had on one of Kamal's shirts and it smelled just like him. I went into the bathroom attached to Kamal's room either he was really into hygiene or he had bitches in and out of here. He had a whole drawer filled with toothbrushes.

"You only get one set of teeth and I've had to pay a lot of money to the dentist for Mina," Kamal said from behind me. I looked in the bathroom mirror and he was just standing there. Anybody else I would not have wanted them to see me looking like how I am. Hair all over my head, crust in my eyes and breathe on fire but he still looked at me the same way he did when I first got here.

"That brush is Mina's, she won't stay the fuck out of here."

I looked over at the shower, "I would come in here too if I was her."

"I got you something to wear today, you can go home tonight," Kamal said and walked away.

I needed to be getting on the highway and taking my ass to work, but I wasn't. I like the attention and time that K was putting into this and I wasn't ready to go back to my regular life just yet. I looked at my phone and Fat Ricky had called, but what he wanted was all I had left. Unless some work fell into my lap I wasn't fucking with anybody but Shod so until he comes home. I'll have to live off my weekly paycheck and pills which I'm not trying to do! I jumped in the shower as the water hit me in my face; I just feel that this is too good to be true. This nigga probably got five bitches throughout the city and here I am starting to like this nigga.

"Girrrll, you take forever to get ready, like K. Hurry up and eat so we can go shopping. K in a good mood, Monday's is K day so he doesn't usually do anything for nobody. You need to move in if K wakes up feeling like this cuz you here." Mina said.

"Shut up Ahmina and stay out my business," K said as he walked in the room, with Hope.

"She's always smiling and happy," I said.

"That's because she likes you, if she didn't she would just scream and holler until you left," K said and Mina co-signed.

K sat next to me in the breakfast nook and Hope was reaching out for me. So I got her, I assumed that she just wanted some of my food but she just sat on my lap singing and clapping while I ate. I could feel Kamal staring at me, "wassup?" I asked.

"Are you really done with ol boy?" K asked. My lips said, yea but I wasn't sure about that yet.

I just still don't believe that a man like Kamal wants me and only me. I know what to expect from Deontae. He isn't shit, but I know that and I know what comes with fucking with him. I have to weigh my options and make sure that it is worth it to leave Deontae for good.

K told me they were moving and a Company was coming to pack everything up in a few hours. Before we went to the mall, we had to go to the new place. I never met a man that had his shit together like Kamal yea, he does what he does as a means of income but he's not just in the way taking up space. He's really getting money. I love the fact that K isn't dumb and he knows more than the streets! He has more than one home, that he owns and he takes care of Hope and Mina by himself.

KURUPT

I SAID I wanted to take things slow and make sure that Kai was the one, but I didn't want her to leave. Gotti told me she was loyal from what he saw from being around her. So that is definitely a plus. I had to leave again because Red never showed up to take his momma to dialysis this morning. E and Gotti were in the streets looking for him so he'd be got soon.

"You Alright?" Kai asked.

"Yea, I'm good baby."

"Let, Kai eat in peace, so we can go," I said picking up Hope.

* * *

MINA GRABBED kai arm and damn near dragged her into Louis Vuitton. I had Hope and kept walking around. I have been damn near having to make her let me pay for her stuff since we been here. I appreciate that she's not the type of woman that wants a nigga to do everything, but it would be nice if she would let me do this petty shit without an attitude. My phone was vibrating, it was Alice.

"What's going on momma?"

"Ready to get the fuck out of here. When y'all come, up here on Wednesday bring me candy."

Alice complained about her sponsor and the people in the rehab with her. I haven't discussed Alice's situation with Kai and shit if she can't let a nigga buy her a bag without it being an issue we might not be able to go any further than this anyway.

"Momma why would a woman not let me do stuff for her?"

"She's used to fucking with broke ass niggas, that either hasn't done nothing for her or when they have they throw it in her face? You must have a new girl because Quaneisha hoe ass will gladly take anything anybody gives her."

"I don't know about her being my girl, but I am feeling her. I'm not about to pay for something some other nigga did to her doe."

Alice started out just wanting candy, now she got a whole list of shit that she wants. I listened to her as I thought if I needed to step back from Kai and see if this is really what she wanted. Kai and Mina came into Gucci as I was standing at the counter, being checked out. Alice asked to speak to Mina, so I handed her the phone. We made our way out the store. Mina had taken Hope from me and went ahead.

"Kai am I doing too much too soon?"

"No, I mean yea. I'm just not used to all this and I don't want it thrown in my face later that —" Kai attempted to say before I cut her off.

"I would never do anything like that and you can't hold it against me that I'm not a broke ass nigga. If you can't handle the mall, I don't know how we are going get anywhere."

Kai didn't say anything; she grabbed my arm and held onto it tight. I'm going to take that as she understands for right now. As we made it to the car, I decided I needed to tell her who I really was before we go any further.

KAI MORAE

As we drove back to Kamal's and Gina was calling. I just couldn't help but think about what K said to me at the mall. I know that he meant everything he said. I was going to either have to get with it or leave him alone.

"Where are you going?" Mina asked.

"By the new house, K said grabbing my hand.

"All the way out here in Castle Rock; why we have to move way out here?"

At that point, I decided that I was going to let K in all the way and push my insecurities to the side and let a real nigga make it right. Kamal's place is really nice, but this neighborhood that is even better. I don't know who was more impressed Mina or me. Every house we passed by they just got better. As Jay-z's "Moonlight" cane through the speakers of the truck, you would have thought that it was their family's theme song the way they all sing along word for word. I had to look back because even Hope knew every word. It felt like we had been driving forever but we finally stopped in front of the best one. It was away from all the others. There was a lot more distance between this one and the other homes.

"Come on Kai," Kamal said while holding passenger side door open.

Mina had already run ahead into the home. Kamal was going out of his way to make me a part of his world and putting in all the effort and time than anybody else would love to have. Hope was reaching out for me, so I grabbed her out of K's arms and he grabbed my hand pulling me towards the front door.

Kamal had clearly been here before he wasn't as amazed as I and Mina were. As we walked through the home Mina screamed: "This is my room, Kamal!" K didn't respond; I know that he'll do anything to make Hope of Mina happy. So whatever Mina wanted she was going to get and she already knew that. Each room is better than the next. As we got to the end of the hall on the second floor Kamal grabbed Hope, she had fallen asleep.

"Kai, I have to tell you something."

"What's up K?"

Awl shit I thought to myself I knew it was something wrong with this nigga. I sat down, in the chair that was in the room, preparing myself for the worst. Mina was standing in the doorway. Whatever the fuck he was about to tell me I'm sure Mina already knows anyway.

"I'm a gangsta", Kamal said.

"O, I know you sell drugs," I said.

Mina and Kamal both started laughing. Mina grabbed Hope from Kamal and left out the room. Kamal was still laughing, shit I must have been missing something.

"Yea, but I'm not standing on the corner or sitting in no traps. there are times when I have to leave town and handle shit. I'm just telling you this now, so there are no issues later on down the line. You know now what you're getting yourself into."

"Okay, I'm not sure what you want me to say to that."

"I just need to know that it's not going to be an issue for you."

"It won't be, I'm down to ride but I just always had the wrong nigga driving," I said, walking up on Kamal.

Once, I got in front of him, he wrapped his arms around me and at that moment I realized this is where I wanted to be. Nothing else mattered and it anywhere else that I'd rather be. Kamal kissed me and I eased my tongue in his mouth. Just when I was ready for him to rip off this PINK jogging suit; we were interrupted.

"Dad!" Hope screamed.

"Kamal this lady down here, for you to sign some more papers!" Mina screamed.

I attempted to pull away from K and he just held onto me tighter. "K, go down there and talk to the la−" I attempted to say before K, bit my lip. Mina and Hope kept screaming for Kamal, so we were going to have to wait. I need, to head home anyways I have to go to work tomorrow.

KAI MORAE

"You ou need to just pop that pussy for a real nigga. I mean you popped it for Deontae broke ass." Katrina said.

I rolled my eyes, shit she was right but I even though everything had been going perfect it's been a little over a month since we've been seeing each other it's like everything is going too good and something bad is going to happen soon. I pushed those thoughts to the back of my head and decided I was going to enjoy tonight with my girls and worry about my love life tomorrow.

As we pulled up to Cariya's I got a text from K, **I want you to meet my mom.** I said okay and that I couldn't wait to meet her. That was all bullshit, I hate nigga mommas, I do not want to meet her and she's never done anything to me and I don't even know her. I need a fucking orphan!

I'm not trying to meet anybody's momma not just his. My experiences with mommas are never good. I told him I would meet her. We were going to Cariya's to pregame before we go out tonight. Cariya, unlike Katrina, understands why I'm hesitant with K. Katrina thinks because he's getting money nothing else matter. My phone started ringing it was Deontae's sister Jalisa. I haven't talked to them in a minute so I answered.

"Dang, so you acting funny acting!"

"Naw, I have just been working and going to school."

She was trying to be too damn friendly. She was asking too many questions instead of just getting to what the fuck she really wanted. I've needed to change my number, so that's going to have to happen soon.

"Well, my brother wants you to come and see him."

"Alright, I'll go and see him."

I wanted to know what the fuck he could want from me. I got screenshots of Facebook arguments between bitches arguing about him. I haven't written him, sent him any money and this is the first time I talked to any of his people. I rushed her ass off the phone so I could get back to my night off and the bottle that was now in my hand. Cariya and Katrina talking so much shit and I know Jalisa can hear them.

"I know you didn't say you are going to see Deontae!" Katrina yelled, standing over me.

She's been against Deontae and me from the beginning so this is not surprising. He doesn't have enough money for me either and I'm not even money hungry. I didn't waste my time responding I just took the bottle to the head. So we could get ready and go.

* * *

As WE PULLED up to Epernay I was already ready to go. I didn't want to go out, but they did. I would have rather been with K. Luckily it wasn't a long wait in line so we got right in. Katrina was fucked up staggering bumping into people and shit. This bitch does not know how to act. Cariya is getting irritated by Katrina I could already tell. As we made our way to our table, somebody grabbed my arm, I looked up and it was Memphis. I snatched away and he threw his hands up "damn my bad baby."

I rolled my eyes and turned to walk away, I could still smell the Axe that he was drenched in and the twist off cap liquor coming from his pores, so I knew he was behind me.

"I'm sorry about what happened; I would have never shot you, but that nigga gotta go." Memphis said, running his hand over his neck.

I had sat down at the table. I never told Katrina what happened because I didn't want to hear her mouth. I told Cariya though, so she didn't look as confused as Katrina did. It didn't matter to me either way because Deontae was some other bitch's problem, not mine. I just looked at him; I didn't have shit to say to him. He knew better than to sit down he just stood at the table looking dumb.

"Now that he out the picture you should give me chance, I can show you how a real nigga can take care of you."

"Muthafucka, she's not interested!" E said as he walked up.

Memphis got the fuck on and didn't even attempt to say anything else. The few times I've been around E I know that he is crazy as fuck and clearly Memphis either knows too or didn't want to find out.

"Thanks."

"No problem you fam."

"What's yo name?" E asked.

"I'm Katrina."

I grabbed Cariya's arm and made our way to the dance floor. E ain't shit and neither is Katrina. I do not want to be a witness to shit because when Envii finds out she'll beat the fuck out of both of them. I'm not getting in their shit. Now that Memphis knows to keep his distance I'm going to try to enjoy myself.

* * *

"Did you have fun with yo girls?" K asked.

"Yea, it was cool."

I was in the kitchen cooking and he was sitting at the table reading the newspaper. The girls were at home. He came down this morning. I just hoped E didn't bring up Memphis because I just don't want to even talk about it. I made bacon, sausage, eggs, grits, and biscuits. If I wasn't at work or school I was usually with K and I liked it that way. He uplifts me and supports everything I do. It's nice to have someone around that had your back the whole way and wants nothing from you but the same in return.

"Let's go out of town for a few days," K said.

"Where?"

"Wherever you want to go."

I was still getting used to that. Whatever I wanted I can get. Nothing is too big or small for him to come through and handle. He doesn't say it anymore but I know he gets mad when I don't want him to handle everything. If I have a bill on the fridge, so I can remember to pay it. K will just go pay it. I never had that before and I don't want to become dependent on anyone even K.

"I don't care, where ever you want to go, "I said.

I'm not picky and I don't want much. K, on the other hand, is picky as fuck. One generation out the projects and booshy as hell. He has an opinion about everything. So I know he already knows where he wants to go.

"Alright, well take off next week and I'll get everything together baby."

KURUPT

"YOU COULD JUST STOP WORKING and focus on school Kai," I said, taking our plates to the kitchen.

Kai didn't respond, I understand her being independent but she doesn't have to work. She at the house all the time anyway, she can move out of here and just come live with me. I don't understand why she insists on working and keeping this apartment.

"I know you heard me, Kai."

I grabbed her by her hand and led the way to the living room. I wasn't going to press the issue now, but real soon I will be. I'm really feeling Kai and Hope and Mina like her too, so she stuck with us. Kai straddled my lap. She still hasn't given me any and it's killing me. I'm going to wait until she ready, but damn how long do I have to fucking wait! I wonder if she just playing me until that nigga gets out. Sometimes I wonder if that is why it seems she's always hesitating when it comes to us.

"Baby, what do you want from us?" I asked.

"I just want to be happy and for us to be together forever."

"All you have to do is love me and be loyal and whatever you want or need from me you got that no questions—" I attempted to say before Kai kissed me.

Being around Kai, in this short amount of time has made me start thinking about a lot of things. Hope is getting older and I been ready to settle down and to have her to come home to would be perfect. Kai has brought me peace and no bullshit. When I call or text, she gets right back; she focused on bettering herself and actually putting in the work to get shit done. All my free time has been going to her, Hope and Mina. She doesn't blow up my phone when I'm on the road and she's just the fucking truth! The fact that she doesn't ask for anything and I'm willing and ready to give her anything means a lot to a man like me.

There is just one thing Kai is killing me with this lock on the pussy. I know I have to wait until she's ready and I respect that, but damn. I just want to know what we are waiting for. Kai stopped kissing me and got off my lap. Just when I thought today might be the day.

"I'm about to get dressed."

"Alright," I said biting my lip.

I texted Quan, I still been trying to get with her, so I can get rid of her and that nigga Red must have gone missing because we haven't been able to get with him either. We have to go meet with Lady H tomorrow. I know she knows about this shit and she's going to want shit handled quick and fast. My phone started vibrating, so I figured it was Quan but it was Mina telling me about a bag she just has to have. I didn't respond fast enough so now, she's calling.

"K, can I get it?"

"Fuck no, what is Hope doing?"

"She's sitting right here watching Mickey Mouse, Please!"

I never tell Mina, no, but she still insists on asking me instead of just going to get it. All that she does for Hope, she can get whatever she wants and she already knows that. All she needs to be worried about is school and everything else is irrelevant.

"Yes, Mina get the damn bag and quit yelling in my ear. Make sure you feed my baby and get Kai one too."

"Naw, I'm going to let Hope starve and why Kai gotta to get my bag?"

"Bye Ahmina, feed my baby and get my boo a bag."

Kai came back into the room and now my momma calling. I've been going to see her every week and Re-Re has been being supportive too. Mina was hesitating but I know that even though we never talked about her she missed our mom. Every kid wants their mom and I just wonder how I'm going explain to Hope one day about Quita.

"Yes, momma."

"What are you doing? Are you still coming up here today?"

"I'm at Kai's —" I attempted to say before she cut me off.

"You must like her. Does she have some hair? Is she a hoe?"

Alice and her damn questions she hasn't even given me a chance to answer any of them. I had told my mom about Kai, but I didn't tell her enough I guess because she still asking all these damn questions. Kai had snuggled up next to me on the couch. I know she could hear Alice. She had changed subjects talking about the people in the rehab.

"Alright, momma I'll be up there in a minute."

"Don't try and rush me off the phone because you're with that girl and don't forget my candy," my momma said and then she hung up on me.

"What are you doing today?" I asked.

"Nothing much, probably go get my nails and feet done and come back here and finish reading."

I didn't want to leave, but I needed to get up there to see my momma. Kai never trips and is always understands every damn thing. Kai got up putting on her jacket and shoes. Even in a Nike jogging suit, she is the baddest and I love everything about her.

"Call me after, you get done I should be home by then."

"Alright, I will," Kai said poking out her lip.

I wrapped my arms around her and kissed her. Kai is a really good woman and I'm glad she finally quit playing and given me a chance. I'm willing to change the game and make it all about her as long as she does what I need her to do. We continued, to kiss until Kai pulled away.

"Go see your mom."

"Alright yellow, if you don't call me I'll be back over here."

Bad News daughter has a gymnastics competition today. Gotti has something to do and E is missing so I'm sure he's a bitch. Bad News wouldn't be making his rounds so I decided to go and make sure that everybody is playing their part so that things are being handled properly. As I made my way around everything had been damn near perfect, but my last stop this nigga was pissing me the fuck off. He was yelling orders from his car parked across the street loud enough for everybody in the neighborhood to hear. I watched from a distance as long as I could before I jumped out of my car and made my way over to Boo. He was too busy talking on his phone and pulling out money to impress the bitch going into the store to notice me. Every other nigga noticed me and got the fuck on. He jumped inside of his all-black Maserati and I jumped in the passager seat.

"What the fuck are you..." Boo attempted to say while reaching for his heat. I have mine already to his head.

"You can go on head and go home for the day."

"My bad, I didn't know that was you, Kurupt," Boo said while throwing up his hands but my gun was still pointed at his head.

If I don't do it right now, eventually it will still need to be done. He's bad for business and the last thing I need is a muthafucka like him fucking up shit for me. Loose links break chains.

"I fucked up, it's cold out there," Boo pleaded again, but it didn't matter.

It is cold that's why if the weather prevents him from playing his part than I need to find somebody that can get shit done in winter, summer, spring or fall! If snow is going to prevent you from getting money then I suggest you move to a tropical environment. I didn't have shit else to say; I opened the door so I could get out before I put two bullets inside of Boo's skull. His brains were splattered over the dashboard and Durt pulled up behind Boo's car as I shut the door.

Durt jumped out the passenger side and got into Boo's car, while rolling his lifeless body over to the passenger seat and hoping in the driver seat and made his way to my shop.

As Durt pulled off, Prodigy made his way over to me. Time doesn't permit me to make these rounds daily but I had noticed Prodigy several times. The way he talks and handles himself reminds me a lot of Bad News.

"You ready?" I asked.

"Yea," Prodigy answered.

This is a business it's not personal. Who knows what the fuck Boo yelled across the street before I got here? I did all of us a favor and clearly, none of these niggas were concerned about the fate of Boo because they all just made their back to their positions like nothing just happened. I spit at Prodigy for a second and made my way home to get myself together so I could go see my momma.

KAI MORAE

I DIDN'T WANT K to leave but I understand he has to go and see his mom. Something in me wanted to say fuck this apartment and Netflix and make way to K's. I'm just not sure if I'm ready yet, but K is here and ready. I made my way around the corner to Katrina's. Even though she knows I'm coming she'll be still getting ready when I get there. I let myself in since she didn't answer.

"Hurry up, Katrina so we can go!" I yelled.

We had appointments to get our nails done and I wasn't trying to be late. This bitch is late to everything. She disappeared last night and I know she left with E and I don't want anything to do with that. E is definitely married and I told Katrina that and she doesn't give not one fucks.

"Well, I'm a little exhausted because I had a great night with Enforcer last night."

"Bitch when Envii, finds out she going to fuck you and E up."

We made our way out of Katrina's and to my car. She was still talking about E and I already know what she wanted from a nigga; money and dick and in that order. She isn't going to ever change. I love Katrina and she's one of the very few friends that I have but I wish she wasn't so damn messy. I have to be around Envii and Enforcer and I wouldn't want to be around somebody whose best friend is fucking my husband. I just rolled my eyes and said yea and agreed with everything Katrina was saying.

"I'm going to be at Sunday dinners soon bitch! He been texting me all morning and wants to see me again already bitch!"

"He's not going to bring you to Sunday dinner bitch. Let's not go there and you need to just leave him alone. Don't say I didn't try to tell you."

We finally made it to the nail shop and Katrina just kept on talking about E, now she's referring to him as a blessing. This bitch really has no sense at all. I can't imagine that E did anything but fuck her that would make her feel like she is that bitch today.

"My boo, is coming up here to see me, let me go check my make-up," Katrina said as she got up.

"I'm coming to you as a woman and I'm going to tell you this one time only," A woman said while walking in my direction.

I looked around because I know damn well she isn't talking to me. The bitches all around the shop were pulling out their phones so I know I was being recorded. I've never seen this bitch before and there is no way she coming to me as a woman about anything. I took a breath and sat back in the chair I was sitting in for my pedicure and adjusted the massage settings.

"Excuse me do I know you?" I asked once the lady made her way in front of me.

"No, but you do know my man Kamal. My name is Quaneisha and Kamal is mine. Whatever you think yall had is over. He will always be my man and I'm the one at Sunday dinners with his family and helping him raise his daughter."

I couldn't help but laugh because unless there is more than on Sunday on the calendar that I don't know about she hasn't been to a Sunday dinner here lately. She must be a bitch that just can't let go. Kamal is that nigga and I'm sure it's some more Quaneisha out here.

"O so, you think it's funny. He told you he was going to see his mom in rehab right, but he's lying in my bed right now."

"Is he? Well, he's calling me right now from yo bed, so let's see what he has to say."

Quaneisha turned to walk away quickly, but it was too late for that. I was on her ass, following her out the shop. I'm mad because she knows something and she clearly had been talking to Kamal to know his whereabouts for the day.

"Yea, this Quaneisha bitch just came up to me in the nail shop telling me to stay away from her man and telling me you are in her bed right now."

K was saying something but I wasn't listening and Quaneisha was now running out of the shop. Something wasn't right about this situation because if my man was on the phone I would want to talk to him on the other bitches phone because that would answer a lot of questions that would be keeping me up at night. From the bags, under Quaneisha's eyes, she hasn't been getting much sleep.

"Kai Morae! Are you listening to me?" K screamed in my ear.

I stopped following in behind Quaneisha and turned around to make my way back in the shop. I hung up on K; I didn't have anything to say not right now. "Let me get the door for you," Somebody said from behind me. I turned around and it was E. I just shook my head at him and E opened the door.

"Hi, nice to see you Kai; what the fuck did Quaneisha say to you?" E asked.

I just kept walking, it was none of E's concern and he must have seen her in the parking lot and I know my facial expression is telling him I'm mad as hell. I was ready to get the fuck out of here and go home. Everybody in the shop was staring at me and I was so damn mad, I left my purse on the chair. I checked it to make sure all my money and cards were still in my purse.

"Bitch what happened? What did that bitch say to you?" Katrina asked, jumping in my face.

E was standing there trying to hear what I was going to say too. Goddess walked into the nail shop. She is a bad bitch and everybody was staring at her. Goddess is caramel, tall, with long straight black hair and her personality is the exact opposite from Envii. I've only met her once, she doesn't really come around too often, but I don't know why.

"What's up brother and Kai?" Goddess said as she walked by.

Goddess and Envii are sisters and the way the E, is slowly moving the fuck away from Katrina he knows that if Goddess finds out anything Envii will be up here real quick. Katrina tried to grab E's arm and he was shoeing her away like a fly. Goddesses back was turned towards us, she was looking at the polish on the other side of the room.

"Come outside in five minutes," E whispered and got the fuck out the shop before Goddess turned around.

QUANEISHA

"**W**hy are you following this car?" Ra-Ray asked again.

I'm sick of this bitch. I haven't answered the first five times and I'm not answering now. I needed to find out who this bitch is that has K ignoring me and now he can't fuck with me anymore. Yea I didn't run to Mina's assistance but we got history. This bitch driving this fucked up ass car. Her hair is basic, clothes basic and I know her pussy don't get as wet as mines. I noticed her giving Ray-Ray bum ass a ride. We were now stopped at the gas station. I know she's not going to see Kurupt, it's Sunday. He only spends time with his family on Sunday.

"What did Kai do to you?" Ray-Ray asked.

"You know her? Who does she fuck with?"

Now we could talk I needed to know everything she knows about this bitch. I needed to get the fuck away from Red and Ray-Ray. I'm sick of both of them. Red can't stay on to save his life and his infatuation with wanting to be K is getting so bad it's pathetic. Damn all day long all he does is talk about K. I'm not sure why or when the beef even started. K has never even mentioned him in all the time I've known him. Red beefing with himself because Kurupt hasn't lost any sleep because of Red.

"Kai fuck with this nigga name Deontae, I use to fuck with. He locked up right now doe. She stays out the way she be with this messy hoe name Katrina. She smart, she is college and shit."

"Can you get a message to Deontae and get somebody to have him call you?"

"Yup, I'll call his sister my bitch Jalisa."

That didn't take any effort in the meantime I'm following this bitch to see where her next stop is and it better not be to Kurupt! As soon as she pulled off, I was on her ass and every time she switched lanes so did I.

Kai was headed to a neighborhood that wasn't Kurupt's unless he moved. She from the same neighborhood as Ray-Ray she doesn't have enough money to live out here. Not driving that car and security is not letting me through the gate without a code.

"Fuck!" I screamed, hitting the steering wheel.

"Jalisa said she'll call me on three-way when he calls her later on."

Finally, this bitch was good for something! I made my way to the house, so I could get her rat ass out my car and think. I need a blunt, wine and some head.

KAI

"Mina, get out that room, so Hope will stop going in there before I kick both of y'all out!" K said while leading me down the hall.

"Kai!" Hope yelled running towards us.

"Hey girl!"

I picked her up and made my way down the hall to meet K's mom. I didn't want to meet her. I was doing this for K and only K.

"Momma this is Kai and Kai, this is Alice," K said.

"Hi, how are you doing?" Alice said.

"Good, how are you? Nice to meet you."

Out of all the people that could have been his mom old lady Alice, is his mom. I can kiss this goodbye because once he finds out I was serving his mom were done! I sat down and started gulping down my bottle of water. Hope made her way out the room.

"Momma don't get on Kai, nerves I'll be right back," K said as he walked out the room.

"Bitch breathe, I'm not going to tell Kamal I know you," Alice said as she flopped down next to me.

I can say a lot of things about my customers but I can say that Alice means what she says when she says it. She's not messy or one that has lied to me ever, so I can believe her. I think that I should still tell K because I would want to know something like that. I know how he feels about family so I can only imagine how this is going to turn out. K and I just barely got back right after that incident with Quaneisha at the nail shop.

"She ain't getting on your nerves is she?" K asked as he walked in the room.

"No muthafucka I'm not getting on her nerves. Is my food done?" Alice asked as she walked out the room.

Kamal sat down beside me wrapping his arms around me and started kissing my neck.

"Kai!" Hope screamed from down the hallway.

I was trying to get up to go see what she wanted and K was holding on tight to me. Whenever I'm around him I can't help but smile, laugh and have a better time than last time.

"K, I'll be right back."

"You better," K said as he let me go and slapped my ass.

"Kai!" Hope screamed again.

"Yes, girlll," I said as I jogged down the hallway to her.

She reached up to me for me to pick her up. I spend so much time here I've grown close to both Hope and Mina. Hope just wanted me to watch cartoons with her. Mina is sitting with Modesty in her room. Mina hardly ever leaves the house and if she does she's with Modesty. I know she gets sick of sitting in this house, but to not hear K's mouth if she is going somewhere besides the mall K doesn't know.

Hopes room is set up with a princess theme and she has custom made furniture with her name or initials on everything. I couldn't sit in that little furniture, so I sat beside Hopes miniature throne chair.

"Kai, look at Mikey."

I had to put my phone down and give Mikey all my attention.

* * *

"KAI, BABY GET UP."

Hope and I had fallen asleep watching TV. I got up and picked up Hope and laid her on her bed. K wrapped his arms around me as we made our way out of Hope's room. I could hear Envia's mouth all the way from upstairs. If she was ever quiet something is definitely wrong. She cussing out E and is getting louder and louder.

"Girl please just shut up for a few minutes. You giving me a damn headache," Alice said as we walked into the room.

Envii didn't give a fuck she was still standing over E going the fuck off. She only stopped to hear what Alice had to say and then got right back to it. I sat down next to Alice and we talked like we normally do. She nosy as hell and always wants to know all of your business. "You done fucking with that broke ass nigga?" Alice asked.

Before I responded K has walked back into the room bringing me a plate.

"Thank you, baby."

"Let me holla at you for a second E," K said on his way back out the room.

"Back up Envii," E said.

Envii is crazy but she backed her ass up so E could get up.

"Is that a no?" Alice asked.

"No, I'm not fucking with him, he in jail. I'm with K, Alice."

"Well at least K got some money because all Deontae can give you is dick and maybe Mc Donald's."

I couldn't help but laugh; she was always talking shit about Deontae so this is nothing new. My phone started ringing it was Jalisa; I sent her ass yo voicemail.

"You should come out with me and Goddess sometimes," Envii said.

"Yea, I will."

Goddess sometimes she comes to Sunday dinner but they must be into it. Goddess and I are friends on social media, but I don't really know her like I do Envii. Envii makes you get to know her and will talk you to death if you sit still long enough. She hasn't stopped talking and Alice is rolling her eyes.

"Kai, can you come here for a second?" Mina asked from the doorway.

She wanted something and she wanted me to ask K for her. I already know, she been having me ask K for stuff the past few weeks. I have never seen him say no to her so she doesn't need my help.

"Kai, will you ask K can I go to the mountains for the weekend?"

"Why can't you ask him? Who are you trying to go with a nigga?"

"No, just Modesty. K got a cabin up there I want is to just stay there. It will be the last thing I ask for this week. Please ask him, Kai." Mina said, pushing me towards the kitchen where K was at with Gotti and Enforcer.

"We gotta go meet with Lady H..." K said as I walked in the room.

"What's Up Baby?"

"Can Mina and Modesty go to the mountains for the weekend?" I said, looking at Gotti and K.

"Mina and Modesty!" K yelled.

"Take Envii, with y'all I'm sick of her I need a break," E whispered.

I just shook my head and Gotti and K started laughing. My phone was ringing and I looked down it was the jail I figured it was Shod, so I answered until the recording said it was Deontae. I just hung up and started to scroll through Instagram turning my phone on silent. Mina and Modesty made their way into the kitchen.

"Why you having Kai, ask me about going up to the cabin?"

"You be tripping and you not gone tell Kai no"

"Yea y'all can go if Kai goes with y'all."

I looked a K; I wasn't trying to go up there with them. I know Mina wasn't just trying to go with Modesty that's just what she told me. E looked so damn happy with the possibility of getting rid of Envii for a few days.

"Will you please go with us, Kai?"

"Yea, I'll go."

"Thank you, Kai!" Mina screamed hugging me.

"No, I thank you, Kai, because you're taking Envii wit y'all," E whispered.

"So now you know this is what happens when you do that," K said.

I rolled my eyes, dealing Envii is going to worse than Modesty and Mina for sure.

"Hun, mommy here's ya baby," Alice said handing me, Hope.

QUANEISHA

So what's up with you and Kai?" I asked.

"That's my bitch she does whatever I say whenever I say," Deontae said.

So I guess he told her to be all up under my nigga. This bitch is a problem and I need her gone. This nigga ain't too smart because he knows nothing about me and he's just willing to talk to me.

"So, it's some big money on the floor all you have to do once you get out is keep yo bitch away from my man."

"Done. What's up with you doe? Yo nigga fucking up I know I can make it right."

I have to play this nigga and it wouldn't take much. He just another broke ass nigga that will do anything for a bag the only thing he didn't know if I had a bag he wouldn't be getting any of it. I'm going to finesse this nigga and get him right where I need him to be. Kai will be back with her broke ass nigga before she knows it. I was too ready for these fifteen minutes to be up on this call.

"I'm going to call you tomorrow," Deontae said.

"Okay, talk to you then."

Red and Ray-Ray we're both looking at me. Red was sitting in a chair across from me and Ray-Ray was rubbing his shoulders. To have two bitches, you should be that nigga a muthafucking Boss! My fine ass alone should be on the arm of somebody that got the spot at the top of the game deserves to have me. Red is just taking up space out here in the way.

"So, have you heard from that bitch nigga Kurupt?"

"No, I'm trying to do some other shit, to get to him."

I tossed, Red my phone because that was next. I have no respect for a nigga that wants to look through a bitch's phone. That's bitch shit and that's why I have two phones. The phone with my shit in it is in my car. Soon I'll be back in the spot I deserve and I will be done with hood polygamy bullshit.

This nigga could barely take care of me and then he wants to bring Ray-Ray broke ass in. She just is literally in the way. She needs to take her ass back to the projects and be a mother to her son. After getting a taste of a real man, it's hell having to be here with a bitch nigga. As I sat on the bed, I just wished that K would bust in here and get me the fuck out of here.

"Bae, it's almost over were getting close," Red said moving my hair and kissing the back of my neck with his dry ass lips.

I looked back at him. Every time he touches me it makes me want Kurupt even more. I just wanted to get away from Red sooner than later. Red made me lose everything. My family will not even talk to me because of him. Red stopped kissing my neck and plopped down on the bed resting his head on these flat ass pillows.

"Come here bae," Red called out for me motioning his hands telling me to come here.

I didn't want him to touch me, kiss me; let alone fuck me. Then he expects me to suck his uncircumcised dick. As I straddled his lap; I have to keep telling myself that this is only temporary.

"I got us. Don't trip," Red said.

This nigga didn't have shit and that's where one of our many problems begins. Red is damn near ripping my bra off. Damn you have had pussy before. You could take yo time and make sure I'm ready. My pussy ain't even damp, let alone wet.

The image in my head of Red' dick just makes want to throw up.

Red was my rubbing titties and that isn't doing a damn thing for me. His dick is throbbing against my pussy, so I got to it. I started at his balls because the nonexistent tip is the worst part. As I tooted my ass up in the air to get in a comfortable position Ray Ray started to eat my pussy from the back. I was sucking the fuck out of Red's balls to put off putting his dick in my mouth as long as I could. Ray Ray's head is just as bad as Red's I'll definitely be using bob tonight. Red was digging so far into my hair he was touching the net that is holding my tracks.

"Bae, swallow it," Red managed to whimper out.

Fuck I thought, to myself. So I thought until red grabbed me by my neck until my face was staring at the ugliest dick I have ever seen in my life. I closed my eyes and licked the top; as I started to taste precum. Ray Ray needs to learn some new ways to move her tongue because she ain't doing shit for me either.

Red started pushing my head as if I didn't know what the fuck I was doing. I didn't need any fucking assistance or lessons with this right here. What the fuck is taking him so long to cum. I pushed his dick as far as it would go down my throat and took it back out and spit all over it, looking up at him. He disgusted me more than his ugly ass dick. I licked up the shaft a few times and his nails were going further and further in my net. I kept moving my ass, hoping Ray Ray would catch a clue that was not out of pleasure and she needed to get the fuck up until it was her turn with Red. The dumb bitch didn't she just kept on licking. Red was coming because he was pumping from the bottom and pulling my damn tracks damn near out. I caught all that shit until it was no more left. I flipped over and Ray Ray dumb ass hit the floor. As I picked up my panties so this broke bitch didn't steal them. Ray Ray was straddling Red I was going to see Bob before I was forced to feel Red's wack ass strokes and nasty ass tongue.

KURUPT

"I'll take Hope with us," Kai said as she came down the stairs with Hopes in her arms.

She had stepped up without me asking her too and the love she has for Hope and Mina is real and genuine with no ulterior motive.

"Are you sure?"

"Yea, Envii bringing Emanii. Don't you have yo go out of town?"

"Yea, but Re-Re was going to keep until I got back, but it's cool she would rather be with you and Mina."

I kissed Kai on the top of her head and Hope was trying to push me back. This work out good because I finally got a hold of Quan so I could handle that too. Kai didn't talk to me for a few days and after I kept popping up at her job she finally agreed to talk to me. I have no intentions of playing with Kai's heart and once Quaneisha is gone for good any insecurities that situation may have put in her will be gone. Quaneisha tried that shit because she doesn't know Kai; she would never try that shit with anybody else. She was going to learn today as soon as Kai and the girls are up in the mountains.

"What time yall leaving?

"2:30, so we need to be leaving soon. Mina and Modesty!"

"Here we come, I'm getting Hope stuff!" Mina yelled down the stairs.

"I already packed it, just get her blanket and that bear!" Kai screamed.

"Are you leaving me for Kai?" I asked.

"Yup, I'll be back. Call uncle E or uncle Gotti," Hope said as I took her out of Kai's arms.

"Thank you so much for taking Envii away from me for a few days!" E yelled as he walked in the front door.

Kai, shaking her head and just walked away. She told me about E and Katrina. E sending that bitch to Miami because we gotta go meet Lady H in Florida. She called Kai early screaming like she hit the lottery but that ain't none of my business. Kai expressed feeling uncomfortable being around Envii and knowing that E fucking Katrina but I done already told her to just stay out that shit.

"Come on Mina and Modesty before y'all get left!"

"Kai, tell Kurupt to leave me the fuck alone!" Mina screamed coming down the stairs.

* * *

I KNOCKED on room 224 that Quaneisha had texted me. I was just about to fucking leave she was taking too long to come to the door. Quaneisha came to the door in burgundy lace lingerie. I played along like I was happy to see her too. The whole time she was playing me. No wonder she gave Alice my damn address. That means that nigga Red knows where I live too. I wish that muthafucka was here E sitting outside his momma's house right now, so when he shows up to take her to dialysis in a few hours he's dead!

Quaneisha really outdid herself for her own death. She had candles burning, Keith sweat playing, rose peddles and champagne.

"I'm really sorry and I want to make it up to you for everything I did Kurupt."

I heard her, but none of that mattered, as she got in her knees in front of me I pulled out my nine and as she looked up at me I pressed it to the center of her forehead. Tears started to fall from her eyes almost instantly she could save them!

"I'm sorry, we can fix this and make things right. I can tell you everything about Red," Quaneisha said while wiping her nose with the back of her hand.

My gun was still pressed against her head" bitch talk." She knew me well enough to know I didn't need to raise my voice to be heard. I could have whispered to a muthafucka and they felt me.

"I never told him anything but where you lived and that you never answered my calls or texts on Sunday's or Monday's," Quaneisha managed to say between sobbing.

"Good girl," I said patting on top of her head before I let off two shots into her skull.

That was all she would have known. Sunday is family day and Monday is my day for me. She never spent the night at my house and was never left in a room unattended for too long. Quan's body smacked the ground and I made my way out. As I walked by the desk attendant I gave her an envelope filled with money, so that she could turn the security cameras back on as soon as I was out the parking lot. The desk attendant is Kelly Gotti's Aunt. She always has looked out, so this morning isn't any different and she's an OG, so I don't have to have any discussion with her she knows exactly what to do.

I went to the house off 29th, to get rid of my clothes and get myself together before going back home.

Quan had already run down all Reds spots down when she finally answered my calls whining and crying about why I chose Kai over her. So there was nothing else that we needed to discuss.

KAI

"DON'T you get sick of screaming and yelling at E, he's never going to be shit," Goddess said.

"You barely say anything and that's yo problem you need to start speaking up more. I got this under control over here." Envii said.

I got up to go check on Hope; she was in our room watching cartoons. Mina should be able to enjoy one weekend without being auntie of the year. Envii and Goddess have been going back in forth for a while now. Envii is the bad sister and Goddess is the angel. Envii is the dope man's wife and she will get crazy on E but she plays her position at all times! Goddess is kind and educated but is definitely a little hood. Whatever problems that Goddess and Gotti have I don't know because Goddess keeps all their problems to herself or she's just not comfortable enough to let me in her business.

"Good night, Kai I have a headache," Goddess said, as I walked back in the living room.

"Nite."

"That bitch just this she so damn perfect she gets on my damn nerves. She got problems just like everybody else and Gotti ain't shit either!" Envii yelled she wanted her sister to hear that last part for sure.

My phone started vibrating. It was K, I'm about to get on the plane I'll call you when I land. Have fun and I miss you yellow.

"Who got you smiling K or that broke nigga E told me about?" Envii asked.

"K, I don't fuck with my ex anymore."

"K really fucks with you because he never brings anybody around us. Especially not Hope; he doesn't play that shit. I still can't believe that hoe Quita. She just up and left when K got locked up and left the baby with Mina."

"I really fuck with K too and I love Hope. Do you know where Quita is at?"

Envii knows everything else so either she knows or she has a theory about where she could be. She took another shot of Remy.

"Girrrll that bitch probably in Texas hoes love to move to Texas thinking they going to have such a better life. Her nigga name is Ray! Bitches love niggas name, Ray! Quita probably doing hair too bitches love to do hair."

I couldn't help but laugh, this bitch done made up an entire career for her too. Envii is crazy she done made up a whole nigga.

Emanii came into the living room. She looks just like E, its crazy how much she looks like him. She's ten and smart as hell. K always talks about how smart she is. Emanii wins awards and spelling bees and shit. You would never think she was Enforcer and Envii's daughter.

"Kai, may I have some juice."

"Yea let me get you some. Are you hungry?" I asked as I got up.

* * *

"NO EVERYBODY IS STILL SLEEPING, but Goddess is up cooking."

"I'm ready for y'all to come back," K said.

"You not even at home. I know y'all going out and partying in Miami. You'll be fine we will be home in two days."

Katrina had been calling me because Enforcer got her out there but hasn't even seen her yet. She not about to talk to me, I'm trying to enjoy my time away. Soon as K called, I hung up on her ass.

"Kai, breakfast is ready, if you're hungry," Goddess said, standing in the doorway in my room.

"Okay thank you here I come."

I finished up talking to K and went downstairs. I wanted to get to know Goddess better, she seemed cool from what I know, but she is hardly ever around so I don't know her like I know Envii.

"I hear you're in school," Goddess said.

"Yea, I'm ready to get this over with, I've tried a few times but I just couldn't get it done but I'm ready and focused now."

"Well if you need any help or anything, you can call me anytime."

"Thanks, I will do that."

Emanii came into the dining room and Goddess jumped up to go make her plate. Even though Envii and Goddess barely get along I've noticed that she and Emanii are very close. I could hear Hope whining, so I jumped up to go get her.

"Mommy, Kai! Get yo baby I'm on vacation!" Mina yelled down the stairs.

"Shut up, Mina. Good morning little baby," I said.

"Who cooked? I'm hungry." Mina said running down the stairs.

"Are you hungry lil baby? Let's go get you something to eat." I said.

Goddess wasn't sitting in the dining room anymore so I went into the living room looking for her. It was nice to be around somebody who has established in her career. Plus she been with Gotti for a while now and she not in the streets acting like Envii. I would never embarrass myself like that let alone K. He probably never would talk to me again if I acted the way Envii does. If Enforcer doesn't text her back fast enough she's going to show her ass and not give one fuck who's around let alone where they're at.

"How long have you been dating Kamal?" Goddess asked.

"A little over a month."

"Genesis told me he really likes you."

I smiled, I don't know if everybody trying to gas me up but I don't need that. I know that K really cares about me because of the effort and time that he puts into us. He's really affectionate and that is something that I never had and I really love that about him. I love everything about K. Other than that incident with Quaneisha, I can't complain about anything else. Everything has been damn near perfect. Even though I told K I was over the Quaneisha shit after we talked about it I'm not. Quaneisha and he had something going on for a nice amount of time and even though he downplayed it saying they were never in a relationship, she's clearly not over it. Is he still fucking her? What if he wakes up and decides that he wants to go back to their situation one day. I can't say that I will take that well down the line.

"Be Loyal and be his peace from the streets and y'all will be just fine. Never let another bitch see you're pressed ever!" Goddess said.

"Let's go skiing!" Envii screamed as she came into the room.

"I'll keep Hope, Kai go. Enjoy yourself. We've been here a million times," Goddess said.

"Are you sure? I don't have to go."

"No, go get ready Kai I got Hope go."

KURUPT

"I'M WITH AUNTIE H," E said.

"She hung right the fuck up no questions asked. I'm going to always say I'm with you." Enforcer said.

"No, the fuck you are not! I love Envii, but I'll cuss her ass the fuck out," Lady Heroine said.

Lady Heroine is E's aunt and we've been doing business with her forever. She doesn't play any fucking games. They call her the black widow, so that name speaks for its self. She ain't ever had to talk to me crazy, but I see how she cuts into her people.

"I wanted y'all here to discuss Quaneisha and Red. I hear Quaneisha was taken care of now, but what's going on with Red?" Lady Heroine asked.

"I got all his places from Quaneisha, I got niggas outside of all of them and when I get the word he'll be gone too," I said.

"I'm trying to figure out which one of my sons will be taking over, so soon I'll be introducing y'all to the chosen one," Lady H said.

"Lady H, Sophia is here to see you," A lieutenant said as he walked in the room.

"Send her in here." Lady H said.

It was a thick, middle-aged Mexican woman. I'm not sure why she would be at our meeting. Gotti and E look just as confused. I looked out at the beach. Lady H's home is beautiful and right on the ocean. It's so quiet out here on Gasparilla Island. I turned back around trying to figure out why Sophia is in here.

"So where is my bracelet?" Lady H asked.

"I really don't know Lady H," Sophia said.

Lady H pulled out a butcher knife. She must be the cleaning lady because she would only be by her jewelry.

Sophia pulled out her pockets. Is she about to cut her up right now? She could have waited until we left for that. Sophia leaned against the conference table, still pleading with Lady Heroine that she didn't have whatever was missing. Sophia laid her hand on the conference table and Lady H chopped off her four fingers in one swift motion.

"I try to help you and this is how you repay me! Because I like you

I'm going to give you three hours to remember where my bracelet is and hurry up and get the fuck out here before you get any more blood on my rug!" Lady H screamed loud enough for everybody on the island to hear her. She is crazy as hell, "back to what I was saying I like the way y'all move together and the money that y'all have bought to the table has been better than expected."

"Lady H, you should spend some time with Envii. Invite her down here for a few days," Enforcer said.

"Muthafucka, do I look like a damn babysitter? I think you should learn how to get yo bitches in their place. Before Envii kills you and one of them dumb ass hoes," Lady Heroine said.

Nothing had changed with our business Lady H just like to check on every so often to make sure everything is all good. With her dope things have been better than good; so I can't complain about her irrational behavior. As long as you ain't fucking her and playing with her heart you're safe or stealing her jewelry. As long as you do right by her, she'll do the same.

* * *

"Are you having fun is Envii getting on yo damn nerves?" I asked Kai.

"She's being her but her she cool. Goddess is cool as fuck too. Hold on Hope wants to talk to you."

I missed them, shit I was ready to go home. Gotti and E, love being down here they trying to hit the clubs and shit but I'd rather be at home. Hope was telling me about the mountains. She's getting so big and so damn smart. I finished up talking to Kai and Hope. E was texting me so we could hit LIV Miami.

KAI MORAE

*a*s I sat looking at my aunt's home all I can think about is all the times she was there for me. Everybody was telling her to let me go to the state but she didn't. I'm not ready to face her yet. Let, me get back home.

"Fuck!" I said as I started my car back up.

I looked across the street at the stop sign I noticed Deontae's uncle Rodney. He just sat at the stop sign, so I know he noticed me. I saw his uncle Josh was in the passenger seat. The way Rodney was staring was making me uncomfortable. I started feeling under my seat for Shod's gun. Then I remembered I left it at the fucking house. Ever since the incident with Memphis, I'm not taking any chances. Since Deontae has been locked up I haven't had any issues. I've known Rodney and Josh all my life. Rodney and my aunt Audrey were married. Rodney tried to warn me about Deontae but I didn't listen. Why the fuck is he still sitting at the stop sign. He finally turned the corner in my direction. Rodney stopped in the middle of the street once he made it where I was parked. I rolled down my window. Its cold as fuck today and it's starting to snow.

"I thought you were yo nigga because of yo coat. I was about shoot up yo car." Rodney said and pulled off.

The way Rodney said it was so casual like it wasn't shit. To that muthafucka it isn't, all he knows is prison and this is the longest he's ever been out. So going back wouldn't be an issue for him. Deontae fucks over in any everybody so I'm not surprised he's looking for him. I'm sure it's either about some money or some dope. Either way, it doesn't have shit to do with me. I just needed to take my ass home.

* * *

"You should just move in," K said.

"Not right now, Soon doe," I said

K and I have been lying on the couch watching TV for hours. I wanted to know was he still fucking with Quaneisha but I didn't want to ask. Shit if he is he not going to admit to me anyways. Ever since the incident at the nail shop, I always think that if K doesn't answer or text back right away he probably with her.

"Have you still been fucking with Quaneisha?" I asked; fuck it I want to know.

"Kai, you don't have to worry about her or no other bitch ever."

I heard him, but I don't know if I believe him or not. I didn't respond; I just will enjoy this while it last.

"Kai, I'm not that nigga I'm not going to lie to you."

"Okay."

I picked up my phone and Gina and Jalisa had both called me. I just put my phone back down. I'm sure they wanted something but those days are behind us. They better get to calling these bitches I keep hearing about.

"I gotta run out for a second. I'll be right back. You want something while I'm out?" K asked.

"Naw, I'm good."

"Kai!" Hope screamed.

I jumped up to go see what Hope wanted, K kissed me on the forehead and made his way out the door. My phone is beeping but I'm sure it's nobody but Gina. Her ass can get to calling back to back if you don't answer.

KURUPT

"WHAT'S UP GOTTI?" I said as I got in his car.

"E got Red," Gotti said, as he pulled away from the house.

That was all I needed to hear nothing else needed to be said. I know this shit with Red would be over soon. That nigga went from being in hiding to just out here tricking on bitches every night. Gotti made his way to the spot where E had Red at.

"Goddess really likes Kai. You know she doesn't like any damn body," Gotti said.

"Damn for real. I mean Kai, is cool as fuck but you know how your wife is."

Goddess is cool as hell, but it took her a while to even come around and even now she barely comes around. I do know that she is all about her business and wants no parts in ours. As we pulled up to the spot, I noticed the car wasn't any of E's cars. Gotti and I looked at each other as we made our way out of the car. I was ready to get this shit over and get back home.

"Envii, would you please just shut the fuck up damn!" E said as we walked into the warehouse.

"No, I won't if you do what the fuck you know you're supposed to do we wouldn't have any problems!" Envii screamed.

Envii was standing in front of what appeared to be Red with her diamond encrusted Glock towards him. E was leaned up against the wall, not too far away. I'm not surprised that Envii is here. She has been very involved in our business from the beginning.

"Why you just didn't stay home and bake some damn cookies or something," Gotti said.

"Nigga I don't bake cookies. That's why Emanii is with her aunt, your wife she bakes cookies, clearly muthafucka. Yo, big ass ain't missed a meal bra."

"Let's focus, right now," I said as I slapped Red with my gun waking him up.

Red is duck taped to the chair and I'm sure all the bruises on his face are from Envii. My wife will not be on the field with me, but it works for them. Red started blinking his eyes. Envii had back up and was in E's face still going off.

"Wake up muthafucka. I don't have all night," I said.

"Fuc—" Red attempted to say, but couldn't catch his breath.

I couldn't help but laugh. This nigga has hated from the beginning but I don't know why. This was way before I ever met Quaneisha. He always just been a broke ass nigga, that want to be given his spot, but if he had it he wouldn't know what to do with it. Not everybody is meant to be in this game and it doesn't take long for that to show to anybody paying attention.

"Fat Ricky is my dad. You started this shit" Red said, in between gasping for air.

"I'm, so sorry to hear that and I'm going to finish it too."

"You can have Quan, I'm done. I won't fuck with yo shit anymore."

I took a few steps back from Red and looked at him. I never realized how much he looked like fat Ricky. I haven't seen that nigga in years and the fact that his son thought he was going to take my spot. Nigga I took fat Ricky's block years ago and I have never had a nigga take nothing from me and I have no intentions of starting now. I shot, Red in between his eyes and his neck snapped back. I let off a few more rounds, just to seal the deal.

"Tell Kai to call me, so we can hang out sometime," Envii said.

"I'm not she will not be hanging with you, Bonnie."

Gotti and I made our way out. E and Envii could finish up what needed to be done. I needed to get back home. All my time and energy can be routed to other shit to make sure that everything else is in place. As we got in the car Gotti said," I need to talk to you K about Goddess, something ain't right."

"What's going on bra?"

"I think she's back getting high, naw nigga I know she is."

Goddess and Envii, both went through a lot of shit growing up. Envii hit the streets hard and Goddess put everything in her education. Goddess started using Heroin when she was thirteen years old.

Gotti told me that she struggled with it for years. By the time we met her she had been clean for over ten years. Gotti and Goddess have been together for about five years and as far as I know, she hadn't touched any drugs since I've known her. She doesn't come around too often, but I just assumed that she was busy working. She's a workaholic.

"Damn, have you talked to her?"

"Naw, but I have to because I can't deal with that shit. She going to have to get some help and I'm going to have to take some time to get shit right."

"Take all the time you need, I got you. You already know that."

Other than Hope, Mina, my momma and Kai my niggas are all I got. We are more than friends and business partners they're closer to me than some of my blood. Anything Gotti or E need they can get. I know that this is hard for Gotti to deal with, but I know that he loves Goddess and it's important that he is there for her as she struggles with her addiction.

"If you need anything Gotti, just let me know."

"Alright, I'll get with you tomorrow once I get everything in order."

Everybody is sleep except, Mina. She's on her phone and sitting in my damn white room. I grabbed me a bottle of water out of the icebox and went and sat with Mina. I needed to check in with her to make sure she was good because I know it's been a lot of changes lately.

"Damn, all these rooms and yall just insist on being in this room."

"K, shut up. I'm grown!"

"Who is that nigga?" I said as I snatched Mina's phone.

She will never tell me about niggas and I don't know why. We talk about everything else, but when I ask about a nigga she won't tell me shit. She needs to talk to me because listening to her dumb ass friends isn't the answer. Whoever Tycoon is, he got some money, but he a young dumb nigga and that shit will bring yo ass down real fast.

"Is this your boyfriend?"

"No, K he's just my friend," Mina said trying to snatch her phone.

"Don't fuck, with any dumb ass nigga. Why don't you date one of them niggas at school? Why you want a thu—"

"Leave Mina alone and come here," Kai said cutting me off standing in the doorway.

I tossed Mina's phone in her lap and got up and made my way over to Kai. I loved coming home and Kai being here. She just needs to move in and never leave already. Kai is cool as fuck and understands me. The little shit means the most to me and she knows that. I wrapped my arms around her waist and she turned around and led the way upstairs.

KAI MORAE

WHEN K, left my mind to begin to run a mile a minute and talking to Katrina didn't make it any better. Mina tried to ensure me of the type of man her brother is but shit she could be telling me anything too. When I heard alarm system saying the front door was opening was the moment I stopped thinking about where he could be. His phone was plugged up to the charger on one of the nightstands I wanted to look at it but I learned from my mistakes. The last time I looked at a niggas phone I learned some shit that I was not expecting or prepared to deal with. Once we made it to K's room he went to get in the shower. I got back in the bed and started watching "The Carmichaels."

* * *

"GIRL, I love E, he is the nigga what I been needing in my life," Katrina said.

This bitch is losing her damn mind. I don't know what the fuck is going on in her head. She has been talking about this nigga referring to him as her "blessing" ever since I got to her house. I had just got out of work and stopped by Katrina's because she been talking shit about she never sees me anymore. I miss K, whenever I'm not with him I want to be and Katina is on my damn nerves.

Knock, knock, knock.

"This probably my baby surprising me!" Katrina said as she made her way to answer the door.

The knocks were getting louder and louder. Whoever the fuck it was about to knock the door down. Something was telling me that it is not E.

"Bitch, its Envii. She got a gun in her hand," Katrina whispered.

Envii was still banging on the door, this bitch was just so in love. Now she's looking at me for the answers. Ain't shit I can say to Envii that's going to keep her off of Katrina's ass. I should have taken my ass home after I left K's.

Pop! Pop! Pop!

Bullets started flying through the living room; luckily none of them were in our direction. I got on the floor and crawled, to the front door. Before I could get to the door more bullets, were coming through the house. Pictures and shit were crashing to the ground all around me.

"You clearly were not told about me and who the fuck I am! Stay the fuck away from E you raggedy broke ass hoe!" Envii screamed, with each word in her last sentence she sent bullets through Katrina's apartment.

"Bitch, if you don't get fucking moving!" I screamed as Katrina sat on the floor crying hysterically rocking herself back and forth. Once I made it to the door, I screamed out for Katrina one last time her ass didn't respond, so I got the fuck out, to try to go and talk to Envii. She had finally stopped shooting. I got my ass up and ran out to the street.

"Kai, tell that bitch to come outside!" Envii screamed once I got to where she was at.

"Envii, please just leave before the police get here."

"I'll be back, I'm getting that bitch!"

KAI MORAE

Tomorrow Deontae gets out and that's all that has been consuming my mind. Maybe because every time I click on social media another bitch is overly excited about his return. Everything has been going perfectly with K and me. I haven't seen Deontae, since the visit and he's called but I still haven't answered. K is out of town and I'm supposed to be going to stay with the girls tomorrow after work. I'm just ready to get out of here and go home.

"Bitch, so tell me why Mike fucking with Nicole," Lay said, walking over to my cubicle.

"For real?"

I wasn't surprised, but I'm not getting in anybody shit. Nicole lived by Alice so I saw Mike over there but that is not my place I'm not a cheaters investigator. I just listened and pretended to be surprised by all the things Lay was saying. Nicole be fucking with everybody so fucking with her, is definitely something temporary so he was the just the new nigga this month. I've known Lay forever so I know she really cares about Mike, that's more of a reason for me not to get involved. Talking to her about Mike was going to make time fly by so I'm all for it. My phone was vibrating on my desk.

It's K, **have a good day at work Yellow. See you in a few days.**

That's what I really loved about K was the little things. Yea he buys me stuff and covers the bill for everything but it was more than just that.

"Bitch, we need to go to Nicole's after work."

"Bitch, how you know he's going to be there doe?"

* * *

"HELLO," I said blinking my eyes trying to concentrate on the clock to see what time it is.

"Baby, I'm home!" Deontae yelled in my ear.

"Welcome home. Shouldn't you be calling one of yo girlfriends?"

I was wide awake now. I couldn't help but roll my eyes. Deontae is talking to people in the background. I checked my texts to see if K responded to my text but he hadn't. I stayed up last night drinking with Lay. Going to Nicole's was a waste of time because we saw her going to her house with Toni and not Mike.

"Open the door baby. Did you miss me?"

"I'm not yo baby and we been done for months and that visit just proved to me that we're over."

Then I heard a knock on my front door. So I hung up and got up before he caused a scene and these nosy ass people called the office on me. Out of all the places, he could have gone and he bought his ass here. Kyra had her baby a few days ago so he surely could have gone there. She's been tagging him on Facebook in pictures every day.

I exhaled and opened the door. Deontae was smiling and had picked up some weight, so he was good and chunky. Deontae wrapped his arms around me and hugged me tight; like he never had before.

"Alright, let me go."

"Damn, that's not how you really feel," Deontae said walking around me and into my apartment.

Deontae had walked into the kitchen and was in the icebox like he's at home. I sat on the couch and turned on the TV. I flipped through a few channels and ended up where I normally do Netflix. Deontae flopped down on the couch.

"Look, Kai I know I've done some bullshit in the past, but I'm ready to change and make shit right between us. All the bitches and shit I'm done with that. Tomorrow Omari taking me to look for a job."

The look in Deontae's eyes I had never seen before. He wasn't lying because when he was I could tell. What I didn't understand was why now. I know that jail didn't make him a better person. The whole time I've been dealing with him I wanted him to change but he never did.

"Why now?"

"I realized that I been fucking up and I want us to be back together and start a family."

I got up because my phone was vibrating on the table. It was K, coming home early see you tomorrow baby and I got a surprise for you... was all I was able to see in the preview. I didn't open it because he would be able to see I read it and Deontae was walking up behind me. He hugged me tight from behind. Moving my hair to the side and placing soft kisses on my neck. He turned me around softly and gently.

"I love you, Kai."

"One more chance if you fuck up. We're done forever."

"One more chance, but do you love me?"

"I love you."

I don't know if this is a good idea and going into this with Deontae I have to kiss K goodbye. I can't face him and tell him the truth. With Deontae standing before ready to be the man I always wanted him to be.

I grabbed Deontae's hand and led the way to my room. I could hear my phone beeping, but I acted like I didn't. I will learn to love Deontae and be happy with what I have here right now.

KURUPT

"YEA MINA, wassup? I'm about to get on the plane."

"Have you talked to Kai, she not answering and she was supposed to come over and watch Hope."

"Naw let me call her. I'll call you right back."

I tried to call Kai and it went straight to the voicemail. That's not like her for her not to call and then have her phone turned off.

I texted Mina and told her to call Re-Re. We were just together and everything was all good. So I know I didn't do anything wrong.

"Look at this shit," Gotti said handing me his phone.

It was that nigga Deontae saying he was ready and was trying to get in touch with Gotti. If that nigga out and Kai is missing. I just don't believe she would go back fucking with that nigga.

"You good, everything good with Mina!" Gotti asked.

"Yea she's good."

As soon as I got done with business, I was going to have to get right back home. When we go out of town we usually stay a few days, but I was already planning to go home early. The car I had got her was ready and I wanted to give it to her right away before the snow gets here.

* * *

I TRIED CALLING Kai again but she didn't answer. My momma was calling, I didn't want to hear her fucking mouth today, but I answered.

"Where are you at? What are you doing?"

"I'm out of town momma."

"Where is Kai at?"

"I don't know."

Since we already met with Lady H; I'm getting the fuck out of here right now. My momma will be getting out of rehab soon, but she too damn nosy she can't come to my house. Alice also talks too damn much. I can't deal with that either; damn sure not every day.

"What's wrong with you? Did Kai Morae go back to broke ass Deontae? Is that what the fuck yo problem is?"

"Momma I don't know where she at."

* * *

SOON AS I got off the plane I went straight to Kai's job. It was about time for her to be getting off. I parked next to her car when I saw her coming out I jumped out my truck. She was on her phone so, she must have had me and Mina blocked. Once she looked up and saw me, she rushed whoever she was talking to off the phone.

"Damn, you blocked Ahmina and me."

"Look K, I just can't do this with you and Quan—"

"Don't even worry about it, I wish you the best"

Kai said something as I got in my truck, but it didn't even fucking matter. What's done is done. I'm not chasing anybody and all this is supposedly over a bitch that's dead. I never gave her any reason to question me and think I was trying to play her. If I wasn't handling business I was with her and Hope.

KAI MORAE

I'M at a loss for words; I wanted to get in my car and chase after K but I couldn't. I'm sick of looking at Deontae. I want him out of my house. D, Jalisa, and his momma have all gotten on my damn nerves. It didn't take long for him to be back on the same bullshit. He went from looking for a job to barely leaving the house. I never got sick of being around K. I have been lying saying I have to work. I have been drinking every day just to get through. I never really have been a big weed smoker but I been having to smoke just to go to bed.

After I went missing on K and blocked him and Mina I knew it was over. I was so excited to see K. I just knew he was done with me and would never talk to me again. I called K, but he didn't answer. I unblocked him and Mina. I want to go to his house but I just had to accept the fact that I had fucked up. As tears started to fall, I tried to hold them back but they continued to fall faster and faster. I tried to call K again, but he didn't answer. My phone started vibrating I thought it was K so I just answered.

"Why the fuck did you do my brother like that? Mina yelled in my ear.

"Mina, I fucked up and made a mistake," I said in between my tears.

"Save them fucking tears. I'm on my way to yo house; to get the keys to our house and my brother's car."

Click. Mina hung up in my face. I had forgotten that I had the keys to the car. K let me drive it while my car was in the shop and he never gave the keys back. While D was locked up I spent every moment I could with K. Whenever I wasn't at work or school I was with him. My phone started vibrating again it was D, I sent him to the voice-mail. I forced myself to get in my car and go home, so I would beat Mina there. Even though I need to go home before Mina gets there and I have to hear D's mouth. I can't stop fucking crying and I'm the one to blame. K didn't do anything but treat me how I'm supposed to be treated and be everything in a man that any other woman would kill to have. As I made my way home, I had to get myself together because I'm not having a discussion with D about why I'm crying. Every time I get a notification of my phone I pray that it's K, but again and again it's not him.

When I pulled up to my house, I noticed K's dark blue 2018 Mercedes-Benz X-Class truck. I jumped out, so I could hand her the keys and she could leave. Mina was looking at me like I wasn't shit and her worst enemy. Mina and I had gotten so close and we were like sisters.

"I can't believe you would do my muthafucking brother like that," Mina screamed as she snatched the keys out of my hand.

I wanted to say something, but nothing I can say is going to make this better or fix it. What's done is done. I just turned to walk away and I heard Mina talking shit about me and she was justified in how she felt and everything she was screaming loud enough for the whole apartment complex to hear. All I want to do is go to sleep and forget that any of this ever happened.

"What's wrong with you?"

"I had a long day at work. I'm not feeling good."

KAI MORAE

"*D*o you need anything, Ms. Smith?"

"No, when can I leave?"

"The doctor will be back in with you shortly," the nurse said.

Fuck trying to make me comfortable I'm ready to get the fuck out of here. I have been at Swedish Medical Center for hours. I just want to go home. I came in because my stomach was bothering me. I have been having unbearable cramps but no period. I went to my OBGYN and they told me everything was fine and I wasn't pregnant two weeks ago. Today it was too much for me to take and come in. They had me use the bathroom, so they could run some test and I lost the baby that I didn't even know I was pregnant with. I don't know how I feel and I been calling Deontae and he hasn't answered or returned any of my calls.

Any other time, I call him he answers right away since we've been back together, but today out of all the days he's nowhere to be found. I have been on the phone with Cariya. I can talk to her usually without her judging me. I know she doesn't like Deontae for me but whenever I need to talk to her or need her to be there for me she is. She has been talking about Kamal and I still miss him so much. I haven't seen or talked to him since the day he showed up at my job and that was over a month ago. I have been so depressed, I just been drinking as much as I can as fast as I can. If I'm not at work or school, I'm drinking. A lot of mornings when I go to work I'm still drunk from the night before.

"Kai are you listening," Cariya yelled in my ear.

"Yes, girl I hear you. K isn't thinking about me so, I gotta let that go."

All I want is to talk to Deontae besides go home. The doctor wants me to stay until I naturally pass everything. I hung up with Cariya so I could try to call Deontae again but I got no answer I tried called Gina and Jalisa too. So now the whole damn family ignoring me; Gina calls me a million times a day but can't answer when I call her.

* * *

"Ms. Smith, Ms. Smith. Sorry to wake you, we just need to check you again. I grabbed my phone to see if Deontae had called me back, he hadn't but Kamal had called me and left a message.

I had been sleeping for longer than I thought the sun was coming up. I just hoped that everything was okay so I can go home. I don't know how I feel, I want kids one day but I want to have myself together before I become a mother. Right now wouldn't be a good time. I want Deontae and he talks about us having kids but I'm just not ready. I'm scared that if I have a baby and I'm not ready I'll resent the child. My mom has told me on several occasions that she wished she would have had an abortion. Even though I would never tell my child that I also don't want to regret it and feel stuck. Now that I'm older and have matured I realize that my mom felt like she didn't reach her full potential in life because of me. All her dreams and goals were placed on the back burner and she just gave up on them. After I was out of her household she still didn't follow her dreams so I wasn't the problem.

"So, I want you to make an appointment with your ob-gyn for a checkup. Again, Ms. Smith, we are sorry for your loss."

"Okay, thank you."

The nurse came and took the IV out of my arm. I got up and put on my clothes so I could go home. I tried to call Deontae again and it went straight to the voicemail. I tried to call my aunt Lisa, but she didn't answer. I don't know why I called her because I'm not telling her about my miscarriage I can hear her now.

I gotta go home and get myself together and go talk to my aunt Audrey. I can always count on her to tell me the truth and not judge me. From the beginning, she told me that she couldn't tell me not to fuck with Deontae but to be sure that I'm not a damn fool. I tell her the shit that I can't tell my other aunt. As I walked in my house I instantly got an attitude where the fuck is Deontae at.

My phone started vibrating it was a message from my pill lady. I had to run and see her before I do anything. It's too much money on the floor to let anything come in between that.

KURUPT

"Has everything been alright?"

"Yea, everything is good," Bad News said.

Bad News, handles distribution for us. He is a real loyal nigga and I don't have to question him. He just wants to get money and take care of his family. I met Bad News when he was a little nigga and the way he carried himself and took shit from nobody is what made me fuck with him. I'm meeting with Bad News to check in and make sure he wasn't having any issues.

We made our way to my office in the rental office of my apartment complex.

"You good?" Bad News asked.

"Yea, I'm good."

I'm not but business still has to be handled. The way Lady H ran shit; product came in on a certain day, but always a different location. Lady H people meet with Bad News.

"Some nigga been asking to meet with you, his name is O."

"I don't who that is. What the fuck does he want?" I asked.

"I don't know he been coming around with some bitch. I have never seen him before. This last time I told him to get the fuck off the block and he ain't been back."

I shook my head. O could be the fucking police for all I know and I don't do meeting with muthafuckas I don't know. That's why Bad News never told me until now. I ain't been having any issues on the streets since Red and Mille took an extended nap so I ain't worried.

"You ready for tomorrow?" I asked.

"Yea, I'm leaving after I leave here."

"I'll look into the O nigga, we good.

We finished up discussing our business so I could handle the shit I needed to while I'm in the office. Hope is with her new nanny for a few hours, so I had to make this fast meeting with my employees.

* * *

As I GOT off at my exit E was calling; I will call him back in a minute I just need some time to get my head together. As I pulled up at home, I got the bags out and made my way in the house. It goes from in the sixties to in the thirties real fast around this bitch.

As I opened the door I can hear Hope screaming at the top of her lungs. I made my way to the house to find her. "Hope, look at Mickey," Mina said. They were in my damn white room. I picked up Hope and she kept screaming.

"What's wrong baby?" I asked.

"She wants to call Kai again," Mina said.

Awl shit I thought to myself. Once a week, since Kai been out the picture Hope does this shit. I've tried to call Kai but she didn't answer earlier, but by the time I left Hope had fallen asleep. When she gets to asking for Kai, is usually once but today I guess she really wants to talk to Kai. I walked through the house with Hope and she finally stopped crying after what felt like forever. I laid her down in her play-room downstairs and went to talk to Mina.

"I gotta stay over here for a day or two," E said as he walked into the room.

I didn't even want to know what the fuck he has done to Envii why he ain't at home. Damn, I just don't understand how you love somebody but cheat on them nonstop. I don't get in Envii and E's business but I'm sure it has something to do with a bitch.

"Nigga why you didn't go get a room?" Mina asked.

"I did and Envii got me kicked out of five so far."

Mina started killing herself laughing. I'm not in the mood to deal with Envii's ass tonight. I just hope she doesn't come over here tonight. I can't wait to get on the plane and get the fuck away from here for a few days.

"You called Kai?"

"Yes, earlier when Hope wouldn't stop crying; why?"

"She writing me on Facebook and muthafuckas only do that because she doesn't want anybody to see on her call log that she talked to you."

"I'm good; I don't have shit to say to her now."

Since Kai decided that I was fucking with Quaneisha, she tried to call me that first day but I haven't heard from her since. I didn't want to call her today but for Hope I did. It's going to take some time for Hope to realize Kai isn't coming around anymore. I missed Kai being around even though but I'll get over it. Maybe I'll find somebody in Cali.

Every bitch I ever talked to been coming out the woodworks. I'm not interested in none of them. It's a reason why I stopped fucking with all of them.

"Guess what the fuck Envii did?" Enforcer said.

"What did she do?" I asked.

"She called American Express and changed the password to E is a cheater. I know them fucking people were laughing at me and shit."

Mina and I both started laughing. I'm not surprised because I know Envii, but damn does the credit card company need to know what is going on in your marriage. I know E and I don't think he will ever change and I also know how crazy Envii is so I would think that he would be tired of that shit.

"K don't let him stay here why we're gone Envii going to have the police out here," Mina said.

"I'm going to get Emanii from Gotti's and I'm going with yall," E said.

I know that Hope would love to have all of us there for her birthday, so I ain't tripping I just hope Envii don't show up.

KURUPT

$\mathcal{A}$s we, sang happy birthday to Hope. Seeing how happy she is and the smile on her face makes nothing else matter. All I want is to make sure she's good forever. My phone started vibrating its Gotti. I stepped away so I can see what's going on.

"I didn't want to bother you because I know today is my god baby birthday but somebody ran in Tuesday's."

"Alright, just do what you gotta do I'll be back tomorrow morning."

"Got it. One more thing, Krack wants to talk to you."

I ignored the last comment and told Gotti, I'll see him in the morning. I haven't seen or heard from Kamal "Krack" Wright Sr in forever. When he left Alice he left Mina and I. I'm not tripping and he tried several times to reach out to Mina and me but I didn't have shit to say to him. Krack started to come by and check on Mina. He went from coming around regularly and being a part of Mina's life then he got locked up.

Tuesday just barely got into the house she's in. Tuesday is Envii's people. Whatever they got out of there couldn't have been much. I just want to know who the fuck went in there. I know that Envii is on it. She's a better detective than anybody. She'll be to the bottom of it before my plane lands.

"You have a good birthday baby?"

"Yea!"

I was ready to go to bed. We have been running around Disney Land for two days. I just want to get home to my own bed. It looks like it's about to be some more bullshit I gotta deal with.

* * *

"So what did Tuesday say?" I asked Envii.

"She claims she doesn't know who the fuck it could be. Nobody knows where she moved blah blah. Basically a bunch of bullshit and nothing that can help me," Envii said.

"Where is she at now?"

"Locked in the closet until she can think of a better answer; then she can come out until then that bitch will be there!"

"Locked in the closet up in here?"

"Naw, nigga at her house; I got some niggas standing outside the closet, taking turns rotating."

I had to come and talk to Envii since her and E still tripping with each other. I wish she would let his ass come back. Envii is in charge of the cooking staff and Tuesday. She has been handling cooking for a while but Tuesday her home girl ain't working out. Envii ensured me she had things under control. Envii is so gutta and street; she talks street and bleeds that shit. I wonder sometimes do she know that we not the same and are positions have changed. She insists on still being in the field.

* * *

"What do you mean you looked away and she was gone?" I asked.

"Mr. Wright I am so sorry, I contacted the police and they are here now.

I didn't want to hire help with Hope but with Mina being in school I had too. Gotti had recommended Silvia because her sister has worked for them for years. I'm trying to figure out how you look away long enough for my daughter to be missing.

"Fuck!" I screamed out, as I hit my steering wheel to get home.

I called Gotti and E on three-way.

"Y'all somebody took my baby."

"What the fuck you mean somebody took her?" Gotti screamed.

"Silvia just called talking about she turned away for a second and Hope was gone. I'm on my way home to get the police the fuck out of my house."

"I'm on my way." Gotti and Enforcer said and hung up.

I hired Silvia on the strength of Gotti I just never imagined any shit like this happening. I got to find my baby. Mina's name popped up on my dashboard.

"Yea, Mina wassup?"

"K, I just got home and Silvia and the police are saying someone snatched Hope," Mina said crying.

"I know Mina, I'm on my home now. Don't worry I'm going to find her."

I picked up my speed so I could get home. Hope is the most important thing in my life. I'm all that she has and Silvia has to go. First day back home and this shit happen this can't be life. I know that the police wouldn't be of any help with getting my baby back so I'm going to have to find her my damn self. As I pulled up to my home and jumped out of the car Mina was running out the front door crying hysterically.

"Come on Mina you gotta go back in the house, so I can get these people out my house. I'm going to find Hope and bring her home I promise come on. Gotti and E pulled up, while I was trying to get Mina to go in the house. Gotti snatched Mina; he had no patience he got her in the house.

"We are going to bring Hope back home. You already know that. Envii is out here seeing if anybody knows anything." Enforcer said.

I'm at a loss for words I can't believe that somebody would take my baby. It's some niggas that's mad because of my position in the streets but none of them know where I live. None of them are dumb enough to touch my baby.

I made my way in the house. "Y'all got all the information now y'all can get the fuck out! "Gotti, told the police as I walked in the living room.

"Mr. Wright, we just have one question, do you have any idea who could have done this to your daughter?"

"No."

The officer that was doing the talking was saying something but it didn't matter. I made my way upstairs to change my clothes so I could hit the streets. I could hear Gotti, telling them to get the fuck out.

"Y'all muthafuckas not no help, y'all ain't going to find her!" Gotti screamed.

I threw on an all-black Nike jogging suit and made my way downstairs. Mina can't stay here. I texted Bad News, I know that she'll be good with him until I can find Hope. I'm going to the hood and I'm not leaving until I find out where Hope is.

"Come on Mina," I said.

"We'll meet you over there," Gotti said.

As we made our way out the house, I just thought about who the fuck could have done this. Red and Quaneisha are both dead and I don't know anybody else who would be dumb enough to touch my baby.

"K I'm sorry, this is all my fault," Mina said in between tears.

"Ahmina, this is not your fault. Stop crying, I'm going to find Hope and we'll be back home soon."

"I'm going damn near a hundred and the closer I get to Bad News's the more furious I become. Looking at Mina cry isn't making it any easier. For every tear Mina cries, I'm going to make sure whoever has Hope entire muthafucking family cries just as many. When I pulled up to Bad News's home he was coming out.

I ensured Mina again this wasn't her fault. I caught Bad News up with what's going on and made my way to meet Gotti and E.

As I pulled up to the trap Gotti and E were standing in the curb. E is hitting a blunt hard as hell and Gotti are walking around in damn near a circle so I attempted to prepare myself for the worst. E handed me a piece of paper.

I just want what I'm entitled to have and you can have your daughter. Now that you are in the position you're in its only right that I'm compensated properly. You owe me!

You'll drop off 100,000 in the last bag you bought yo bitch in the trash can underneath the bridge you know what bridge the same bridge you killed Loso under.

At least I let you celebrate her birthday with her and if you want to celebrate anything else with her you'll do what the fuck I say.

With Love, Your worst fucking nightmare

"It was in the mailbox, with this," E said handing me hopes ponytail attached to a pink barrette.

Only one other person besides the niggas standing in front of me knows about Loso and that's Quita.

KAI

As I WALKED into the parking garage leaving out of Cherry Creek mall; I dreaded going back home to Deontae. I thought I saw K in the mall and near knocked over a lady in Nordstrom's trying to get to him only to get up close the man and it was not K. Every day the more depressed I get about this entire situation. Drinking isn't helping and smoking to go to sleep isn't working anymore. I think about Kamal all day and night. I know I fucked up letting him go. I had to hit the panic button on my car to find it. I notice it was a row over in j. I popped my trunk to throw my bags in and I felt something press against my back.

"Move or scream bitch and you'll be dead quicker than planned. If you were my bitch you wouldn't be going through this. Shouldn't have been a dumb bitch," a man's voice said while snatching my purse out of my hand and pushing the barrel of the gun deeper into my back. The man started pushing me in the direction of a suburban. The back passenger door flew open and the nigga with the gun to my back pushing me into the back seat and hit my head on the window. While trying to rub my head I was met by another gun being pressed against my head by a nigga that an hour ago; loved me more than he had ever loved anybody.

I focused my attention to the front seat and focused on the driver its Memphis bitch ass. Shod's gun is in my purse that Memphis threw in the passenger seat. All I can do is pray that I get out of this alive. Deontae lit a cigarette with his free hand, while still pressing his gun to the back of my head. This nigga has been sleeping in my bed every night since he got out and now this is what he does to me.

I can't help but blame myself for being so dumb to believe that he had changed for me and would never hurt me again. All I could do was cry because I brought this upon myself by letting this nigga back into my world.

We made it to this house that I have never been to before I'm just assuming it must be Memphis house. Memphis snatched open the truck door and grabbed me by my hair out the truck. Deontae wasn't far behind and was laughing and joking with Memphis. This nigga is such a fucking clown. What the fuck could Memphis or Deontae's plan on getting out of this? What the fuck are they going to do to me? Memphis still had a tight grip on my hair, as we walked through the kitchen Deontae wasn't behind us anymore, I grabbed a knife that was on the counter and slid it in my pants luckily Memphis didn't catch me.

We walked past a room, with the TV blasting and as Memphis slung open the second room's door. I pulled out the knife and stabbed Memphis in his calf and caused his goofy ass yo drop his gun, but it flew across the room on the tiled floor. As I was trying, to get across the room to the gun "utt unn bitch. Don't move," Deontae said pointing the gun in my direction.

Memphis was screaming like a bitch, the blade was maybe two inches long and it couldn't have done too much damage. I backed up and leaned against the wall. Deontae helped Memphis off the floor and Memphis wobbled over to me and smacked me across the face with his gun.

"Dumb ass bitch."

Deontae and Memphis made their way out the room and locked me in the room from the outside. I looked behind the blinds to see if I could bust out the window but the windows have bars on them. I moved over to the door so I could see if I could hear what they were saying. The Loud ass TV was preventing me from hearing anything. I slid down the wall to the floor. I wasn't going anywhere right now if I wanted to. The TV suddenly cut off and I could hear Memphis clearly by the door.

"I got what you requested I had some other money on the floor. You gotta meet me at my bitches spot on Lima," Memphis said. Memphis had his phone on speaker.

"Muthafucka, do you know how to follow instructions because that was not what you were instructed to do!" The man yelled back.

"Look cuz!" Memphis tried to interject but the man on the phone was not having it.

"No muthafucka you look, sit yo ass there until I find some time."

The door was unlocking, so I scooted back from the door in the other corner. Memphis has tied a shirt around his calf I barely stabbed. I wanted Deontae to look me in my eyes and explain how he could do this to me. Memphis slow ass finally got the door unlocked after a few minutes. I looked down at the blood stains on my shirt and back up at Memphis.

"What the fuck are you in there doing with my bitch," Deontae screamed out.

"Making sure this bitch didn't climb out the window."

I don't know who kidnaps their own bitch. I just wish they would do whatever the fuck they planning to do. Deontae swung open the door, "Okay muthafucka get out of here and we need to talk my boo not answering the phone."

It's getting dark and all I can do is try not to fucking cry. I've cried so much since I've known Deontae. Somebody that was supposed to be different and love me like I deserve to be loved has done nothing but cause me pain and heartache. It got so normal to me with the bitches; I just treated it like part of the game. With any nigga it's going to always be a bitch; I had convinced myself.

I wiped my eye the door is unlocking again. It's Deontae and I can hear by the way he's singing along to Yo Gotti's "Juice", that he's been out there drinking. I don't want to deal with this shit anymore. Deontae hit his Newport and blew the smoke in my direction. How did I ever think that he would love me look at him? He has on the same clothes he had on yesterday.

"What's that nigga number?" Deontae asked.

"What nigga?"

"Kai, don't try to play me, I know you were fucking that nigga Kurupt."

"I don't know what you're talking about. I don't know anybody name Ku—"

Before I could finish, saying Kurupt's name. Deontae was standing over me and snatching me by the collar of my shirt; then threw me to ground so hard that back of my head smacked the tiled floor.

"Bitch, you think I'm playing with you! I'm locked up and you playing house with some other nigga! I got offered a lot of money to kill you and then Quaneisha ended up dead. So you have less than a minute to give me that bitch ass niggas number!"

Even in all the pain, I'm in and I want to get out of here in one piece I will never do anything else to hurt Kamal. I made the decision to let Deontae in my house the night he got out and I'll have to live with the consequences. Deontae was standing over me waiting for the number. He backed up and I got my ass off the floor. Deontae pulled out his phone and attempted to hand it to me. I got as much spit as I could in my mouth and spit in Deontae's face.

"Fuck you bitch I'll never give you Kam—"

Deontae backhanded me so hard I smacked into the window. I took all the strength I never knew I had and attempted to rush Deontae, but to no avail, he hit so hard, on the top of my head, I hit the ground from the blow to my head.

"Wrong answer you stupid bitch! That's why I've been clearing out yo bank accounts. Everything in the apartment is being cleared out as we speak. I let my bitch go through all yo shit and get everything she wanted. She really liked all yo panties. You won't need it anyway!"

Deontae straddled me and began to pistol whip me. I attempted to fight back, but nothing was working and he wasn't letting up. The entire time he was hitting me all in my face with his gun, he continued to remind me how stupid I was. If I never agreed with him about anything I do now. "Open yo fucking mouth!" D screamed with the barrel of the heat pressed against my lips. Blood is starting to blind my vision and the pain I felt initially is starting to fade away too. I tried to catch my breath and everything faded black.

TO BE CONTINUED...

CPSIA information can be obtained
at www.ICGtesting.com
Printed in the USA
LVOW10s2043200318
570524LV00017B/322/P